'...then he ate my ♡ boy entrancers.'

The Confessions of Georgia Nicolson:

Angus, Thongs and Full-Frontal Snogging

'It's OK, I'm Wearing Really Big Knickers!'

'Knocked Out by my Nunga-Nungas'

'Dancing in my Nuddy-Pants'

'...and that's when it fell off in my hand.'

'...then he ate my boy entrancers.'

'...startled by his furry shorts!'

'Luuurve is a many trousered thing...'

Also available on tape and CD:

'...and that's when it fell off in my hand.'

'...then he ate my boy entrancers.'

'...startled by his furry shorts!'

'Luuurve is a many trousered thing...'

'...then he ate my boy entrancers.'

Louise Rennison

HarperCollins *Children's Books*

This edition produced for The Book People Ltd,
Hall Wood Avenue, Haydock, St Helens, WA11 9UL

Find out more about Georgia at www.georgianicolson.com

First published in Great Britain in hardback by HarperCollins *Children's Books* in 2005
First published in Great Britain in paperback by HarperCollins *Children's Books* in 2006
HarperCollins *Children's Books* is a division of HarperCollins*Publishers* Ltd,
77-85 Fulham Palace Road, Hammersmith, London W6 8JB

The HarperCollins *Children's Books* website address is
www.harpercollinschildrensbooks.co.uk

1

ISBN 978-0-00-782480-9

Printed and bound in England by
Clays Ltd, St Ives plc

FSC is a non-profit international organisation established to promote the
responsible management of the world's forests. Products carrying the FSC
label are independently certified to assure consumers that they come
from forests that are managed to meet the social, economic and
ecological needs of present and future generations.

Find out more about HarperCollins and the environment at
www.harpercollins.co.uk/green

*In memory and love for the boys, Oscar Kakoschka and
Arthur Hewlings. God bless.*

Luuurve to the fabbest family a girl could have: Mutti, Vati, Soshie, Johnboy,
Eduardo, Hons, Bibbity, Kimbo, Jolly, Arrow, Millie and the three
remaining chickens. Oh, and welcome to the new diggy dog, Billy. Big
luuurve to the Kiwi-a-gogo and Isle of Wight branches of mayhem. And of
course to the Ace mates: Salty Dog 'of course you haven't broken it you fool
otherwise you couldn't speak' Pringle, Mizz Morgan, Elton, Jimjams,
Guildford calling, Phil and Ruth in Froggland, Jeddbox, Big Fat Bobbins,
Kim 'you can have that one mate' and Sandy, Jools and the Mogul, Lozzer or
Mrs Bridges as I know you, Ian the computer, Jenks, the Hewlings and the
Willans (yes that means you, Candy), Baggy Aggiss and Jo, B and J, Mrs H
and Dan, Alan 'it's not a perm' Davies, Jo Good(ish). And of course to
Stewpot and Sue (please no more jokes about snot). Ay up to the Northern
branch: The Cock, Ann-marie, Katy and Patrick; to the Ace Gang from
Parklands: Rosie, Barbara, Christine C, Linda, Ali and everyone. To Chris
the Organ. Love to the Captain and thank you for letting me use your
togglestick thing. To the St Nicks crew for everything, and in particular to
Dezza the vicar for joy and love and the APPALLING jokes about farting.
(And also to young Phil and family… just love, nothing to do with farting.)
Also a big kiss to the new cruise mates: Bungalow Steve, Dancing Steve,
Simon the Rock God and Adéle, Ironing Tony and Marg. Big luuurve to
Mirella, Dave and the very gorgey Mattea. Thank you to Karen Cunningham
for the lovely frocks and to that Eve the Minx. Finally thank you to everyone
at my work family at HarperCollins: the divine Gillie, fabby Sally Martin
and groovy Sally Gritten; to Caroline and all in the publicity and design
departments – what a beyond marvy job you have all done. Thank you to
Emma at Midas. Bye bye Dom. And as always best love to the Empress. The
end. P.S. Hahahaha you thought I had finally shut up, didn't you? But finally,
thank you to all the fabby readers of my books and all of you who have sent
me such lovely letters (and now and again inscribed thongs…). I luuuurve
you all. I do. I think this is everything… hopefully! Luuurve Lou xxxxxxx.

A Note from Georgia

Dear Chumettes and Chums,

I hope you are all righty as two all righty things. I am, though ONCE AGAIN I am full of exhaustiosity. I have been as busy as a bee (two bees) finishing my latest oeuvre. Oh yes, AND I have been to Hamburger-a-gogo land to see for myself the nation that cannot be bothered to put the "i" in the second half of words... like aluminium, for instance, which those lazy cats spell aluminum. Where would we be if none of us could be bothered to finish off our words properly? I'll tell you where we would be, we would be up shi cree without a padd... that's where.

As you will see, I have reached new heights of sophisticosity in this latest of my oeuvres... boys, lipstick, snogging, snogging, red-bottomosity, jokes about sausages and pants - the list is endless.

I do this only because I love you.

   Georgia

p.s. You don't know what oeuvre means, do you?

p.p.s. You think it is french for eggs, don't you? Like oeuf.

p.p.p.s. You think I have been saying that I have just finished writing my new egg.

p.p.p.p.s. Look it up in the glossary, you lazy minxes, I am far too tired to explain. I have to go and have a lie down on my snogging emporium (bean bag)... zzzzzzzzzzzzz.

Jas, your spaceship has arrived.
Please get in.

Saturday May 7th

Sun shining like a big yellow shining... er... warmey planet on fire thing.

Yesssssssss!

10:05 a.m.

I am quite literally not wandering lonely as a clud, in fact I am treading lightly in the Universe of the Very Nearly Quite Happy.

10:10 a.m.

Something full of miraculosity has happened. My vati, world renowned fool and paid-up member of the Big Twit club, has for once in his entire life accidentally done

9

something good. We are going to Hamburger-a-gogo land! Honestly.

And guess who is there already? Besides a lot of people in huge psychedelic shorts and that bloke who is half-chicken half-colonel. I'll tell you who is there, the Luuurve God is there! Masimo, the Italian Stallion, has gone to visit his olds, leaving me – his new, lurker-free-nearly almost girlfriend – back here in Billy Shakespeare land. So he thinks! Imagine how thrilled he will be when I pop up and say "Howdy!", or whatever it is they say over there.

Let the overseas Snog Fest begin!

10:15 a.m.
The only fly in the ointmosity of life is that Vati is making us go to some crap clown-car convention.

10:20 a.m.
And Uncle Eddie, the baldest man on the planet, is coming with us.

10:25 a.m.
Still, with a bit of luck they will both be arrested for indecent

exposure when they don the leather motoring trousers.

Filled with the *joie de vivre* that is so much a part of my attractive but modest personality, I phoned my bestest pally.

"Jas, it is *mich*, your *sehr guttest* pally. I am calling you *mit wunderbar* news!"

"Oh God. Look, it's only a week till Tom leaves and we were just sorting out my—"

"Jas, I cannot waste time discussing your knicker collection; that is between you and Tom... quite literally... hahahahaha. Do you get it? Do you get it? Knickers... between you and Hunky... do you...?"

But as I should have known from long and tiring experience, it is useless to waste my wit on Jazzy. So I cut to my nub and gist.

"I am going to Hamburger-a-gogo land to meet Masimo the Luuurve God of the universe and beyond. And back."

"No you're not."

"I am."

"How?"

I explained to Jas about the trip and the "Howdy!"

♡ 11

business and everything, but as usual she displayed cold waterosity.

"Where is Masimo going to be in Hamburger-a-gogo land?"

"Ahaha!!!"

"You don't know, do you?"

"Well, not yet, but—"

"He could be anywhere."

"I know, but how big can America be?"

"It's huge."

I laughed. Nothing was going to spoil my peachy mood, let alone swotty nit-picking from Mrs Big Pantaloonies.

I said, "Is it as huge as your gym knickers?"

There was silence.

"Jas, come on, be happy for me."

"It's all very well for you, you can just fancy anyone, but it's different with Tom and me – he's off to Kiwi-a-gogo and I will be left here all on my owney."

Oh good grief.

Hunky is only going to the Land of the Big White Clots for a couple of weeks, but I am still going to have to listen to her moaning and rambling on about the twig-collecting years. However, before she could start raving on about molluscs and cuckoo spit I had a flash of inspirationosity.

"Jas, listen, I have a plan of such geniosity that I have even surprised myself, and might give myself some sort of award."

She didn't even say "What is it?" There was just silence.

I said, "Aren't you even going to ask me what it is, Jas?"

"It's bound to be stupid."

"Oh, cheers, thanks a lot. Well I won't bother you with it then. Even though it involves you and your happiness and is *très bon* and also vair vair *gut. Au revoir. Bonne chance.*"

And I put the phone down. Even Jas cannot spoil my mood. Lalalalalalala.

11:00 a.m.
Better start planning my wardrobe for the Luuurve Trail. What do the Hamburgese wear? Cowboy hats, I suppose.

11:10 a.m.
From what I hear, the Hamburgese are a bit strict hygiene-wise. They're always in the shower and so on. It is to be hoped the customs man doesn't glance inside Libby's bag

and find her night-time blankie, otherwise we will all be buggered.

Oh, so many things to worry about. I think I will have a little zizz to relax myself and then plan my cosmetic routine.

11:11 a.m.

Fat chance.

"Gingey! Gingey, it's meeeeeeee!!! I have just been to the lavatreeeeee!"

My darling sister has kicked open my bedroom door. Hurrah.

11:13 a.m.

Oh good, and she has her "fwends" with her – scuba-diving Barbie, Charlie Horse, a parsnip and Cross-eyed Gordy. Gordy is under house arrest because he has not had the immunisation injections he needs before he is set loose into the wild jungle world of our street. I'd like to see the germ hard enough to take him on.

As they all snuggled comfortably into my bed, the phone rang downstairs and Dad answered it. Vati yelled up, "Georgia, quickly, one of your mates wants to talk rubbish with you for an hour or two on her father's phone."

He has not got the flare of charm, my vati; but on the other hand, what he has got are my tickets to paradise. I must remember that, however ludicrous he is, he has bought me a passage to the Luuurve Machine.

Masimo-a-gogo!!!

I shouted down, "Thank you, Papa, I'll be down immediately, and perhaps later I will entertain you with my piano playing."

We haven't got a piano, but it's the thought that counts.

11:15 a.m.

It was Jazzy Spazzy... tee-hee. I knew she would crumble and want to know my plan.

I said, "So, now do you want to know what my plan is?"

"If you like."

"No Jas, you are still not showing enthusiosity. Try harder."

"I can't."

"Yes, you can. Gird your loins and so on; laugh and the world laughs at you. Come on, you do really want to know my plan, especially as it concerns you, my little hairy pally."

♥

"I'm not hairy."

"Have it your own way, just don't go near any circuses."

"Shut up. Go on then, tell me your plan. Although, unless you are going to give me the money to go to Kiwi-a-gogo with Tom, I don't—"

"Jas, forget about Hunky. He will be too busy lying around in streams with Robbie and hugging marsupials to get up to anything. This is about you and me on the road."

"What road?"

"OK, this is it: when I go to Hamburger-a-gogo... you come with me! Do you see? Driving across America, you and me. We will be like Thelma and Louise!"

"We're not called Thelma and Louise."

"I know that, I am just saying we will be LIKE THEM."

"And we're not American."

"I know that, but I—"

"And neither of us can drive."

Oh dear God.

I said, "Jas, your spaceship has arrived. Please get in."

12:00 p.m.
Ahahaha, Jazzy Spazzy has finally come to her senses (ish).

She has got the scent of funosity in her nostrils and wants to come to Hamburger-a-gogo land. A LOT. So now all we have to do is get our parents to let us. We have a two-pronged plan.

Prong One is a charm offensive on our muttis and vatis to persuade them to let Jas come to America with me. (And also to give her sqillions of squids for spenderoonies.) We are going to be really nice and sweet and listen to them ramble on about the Beatles. I've been practising my pleading and they would have to be made of stone not to give me the entire contents of their wallets.

However, if that fails and they say no, we launch Prong Two: relentless moaning. You know the kind of thing – "All my other friends are allowed to take a mate on holiday with them. How come I am the ONLY person in the universe who is not allowed to take a mate on holiday? Why is it just me? Why? Why oh why oh why?"

"Why?"

"It is sooo unfair."

"Why?"

Outside the front-room door
9:10 p.m.

Right, this is it. I've got my old Teletubbies jimjams on for maximosity on the loveablenosity front.

Front room

Mutti and Vati were on the sofa, curled round each other. I could clearly see Mum's knickers. Erlack. And the curtains were open; anyone could see in. A fat bloke passing by might think it was a brothel for the porkier gentleman. I was going to say that but then I remembered my prongs. So I said, "Good evening, Mother, Father."

Vati said, "How much?" without even looking at me. I laughed attractively.

"Oh, Papa, this is not a material matter, it's to do with friendship and love and—"

Mum said, "I don't care how many of your friends have had their navels pierced. You are not."

"But I—"

But she was still rambling on. "Ditto tattoos."

"But I—"

Vati joined in. "And no, you cannot have a flat in Paris

and a manservant to help with your homework."

Oh, how I nearly laughed. Not. I thought about telling Dad that Rosie said he looked like a brothel madam in his flying helmet and leather jacket, but then I remembered my charm prong and forced a little grin to play around my mouth.

"You two!!! Always kidding about you cheeky minxes! Anyway, all it is really is that, well... you know... Jas is all miz because of Tom going to Kiwi-a-gogo and, well... You know she's my pal, and... well... it would be nice for me if you know... anyway, can she?"

Vati said, "Can she what? Move in? Levitate? What?"

I bit the whatsit. "Can she come with us to Hamburger-a-gogo land?"

10:00 p.m.
Both of our parents have said yes. Unbelievable. Actually, I am not that amazed that Jas's parents said yes because they are, on the whole, not entirely mad. But my parents?

Weird.

It is a miracle for which I would normally thank Jesus. He does seem to be coming up trumps lately. I left Robbie to the

♥ 19

snogging possums but then Jesus sent me a replacement Luuurve God. Hurray! As I say, I would normally thank him personally by laying gifts at his feet (or foot, actually, because one of his feet snapped off), however there is a bit of a problem. Libby has been rifling around in my room and she has nicked my statue of him. I'm afraid Jesus has not quite been himself since. The last time I saw him he had a frock on and Libby was calling him "Sandra", Barbie's new bestest pal.

I don't think God will hold it against us, as he is, after all, a merciful God.

10:10 p.m.

Unless you happen to be that snake in the Garden of Eden. Snakey only asked, "Anyone fancy a bit of apple?" and then God made him crawl around on his belly for eternity. Seems a bit harsh. (Although, as I pointed out to Miss Wilson in our interesting talks in RE, if you were a snake in the first place, being made to crawl around on your belly for the rest of your days doesn't actually seem that bad. Almost like being a snake in fact. I mean this with all reverencosity. I just have a lively mind.)

Oooohhhhh, I am so excited. I can't wait to tell the Ace Gang.

I even kissed my own father AGAIN. This is twice in two days. I must be a bit feverish.

In my bedroom

Libby, Gordy, Sandra and Barbie are all snoozing. They look so lovely and cosy. Our Lord, now heavily rouged, is next to Libby's feet. I don't know why she likes to sleep upside down. Perhaps because it is very scary waking up to see Gordy looking cross-eyed at you.

I looked out the window as I did my alternate nostril breathing. It is vair vair calming. You pinch one nostril closed and then breathe in through the other one, and then hold your breath and let the pinched-up one go and breathe out of that. And then you... well, anyway... all I can say is that the Lord Buddha did it, and he didn't just do it for nothing.

One minute later

I hope it's not like body building. I don't want to be really calm and have massive nostrils.

♥ 21

Two minutes later

For once Mr Next Door has done something nice. He has built a sort of anti-cat fence on the top of his wall made out of barbed wire. Angus will really like it. He gets a bit bored with leaping down on to the Prat Poodles and riding them round. He is the sort of cat who needs a bit of a challenge.

Five minutes later

Oh, here comes Supercat with Naomi. With his head up her bottom as ususal.

One minute later

Aha! He has removed his head and he has seen the new fencey. He luuurves the fencey.

Four minutes later

Old Nimble Paws did this beyond-fabby thing. He did a vertical jump! From standing on the wall he just shot straight up in the air and over the fence.

Five minutes later

Angus is really getting into it now. He leaps over the anti-cat fence and then comes back into our garden by hurling himself through Mr Next Door's rhododendron bush. Excellent! He has made it into a track-and-field event. It is quite literally the Cat Olympics.

Five minutes later

I would prefer it if Naomi stuck to the usual giving of medals ceremony rather than licking Angus's trouser-snake area, but there you are – that is appalling furry tarts for you.

Monday May 9th
The crack of 8:00 a.m.

Crikey. I'd better not get carried away with happiness, otherwise I will be on time for school, or Stalag 14 as I so amusingly call it.

8:25 a.m.

Lolloping along to Jas's place, I had to pass by Mark Big Gob smoking on the corner with his lardy mates. He is quite literally a mouth on legs. Sadly he seems to have recovered his former (crap) self after the minor duffing-up incident with Dave the Laugh.

He just can't help himself, especially when, like now, he has the backup lardy lads with him. As I walked by in a dignified manner, trying not to let anything jiggle about, BG and the lard arses were just ogling my nungas like ogling oglers (if you can imagine the horror of that, and I think you can). Then he licked his lips! Erlack, he was licking his lips at me!

He is so *très* pathetico.

I may have to ask Dave to repeat the duffing-up incident.

Five minutes later

Jas was on her wall. I don't know what she had for breakfast but she has put on about twelve stone. Either that or her knickers have reached elephantine size.

When she jumped down, I saw it was because she had her skirt rolled over so much that she looked like a melon with a head and an annoying fringe in a school uniform.

She said, "My mum and dad want to come round to yours to talk about the arrangements."

"I must rush home and make them normal. Your mum and dad will never let you come with us if Dad happens to be wearing his masonic apron... or his velvet loons that he wears for 'grooving' in. No one in their right mind would let a child of theirs anywhere near him."

Stalag 14

Hawkeye was on glaring duty at the school gates, so Jas had to do a quick dive behind me to let her skirt down. She was fiddling away as we walked along, so to distract Hawkeye with my youth and exuberance I started singing, "Oh, what a beautiful mornin', oh what a—"

"Why are you shuffling along like idiots? Put a spring in your step!"

I started doing a bit of springing for a laugh, but then she said, "Georgia, I have been glancing at your report card and it seems to me a bit of extra tuition wouldn't come amiss."

Bloody *sacré bleu*! I scuttled off to the loos as fast as I could.

Jas was pouting at herself in the mirror as I grumbled on. "'Glancing at your report card'. What kind of life is that? You might as well have a life 'glancing at paint drying' or 'glancing at a cactus not doing anything', or... anyway, it is no kind of a life for a human being. Which is why Hawkeye is so vair vair good at it."

Jas was now upside down under the hand dryer getting

♥ 25

maximum voluminosity into her fringe for the day ahead, but she nodded her head wisely, in an upside-down way.

Assembly

Usual routine: Klingon salute to the Ace Gang, a quick burst of "The Lord is my shepherd" and then some incomprehensible lecture from Slim, our huge headmistress. What is she rambling on about now? She has certainly excelled herself on the fashion front this morning. Polka-dot suit in a lovely subtle orange and black, and sling-back shoes. Parts of her feet have made a desperate bid for freedom out of the sling-back bit. I've never known anyone with fat feet. It's fascinating watching her. When she loses her rag (i.e. every time she speaks to us) every bit of her quivers in a tip-top jelloid way.

"So to my point, girls: achievement. What does it mean today in the modern world? I want you all to consider what achievement really means."

Then she stood there and looked at us. For ages. We stood looking back. She just stood there; we just stood there. Like a staring competition. Good Lord. It went on for ages and ages – you could practically see Miss Stamp's beard growing.

26

Two centuries later, Slim said, "How many of us could put our hands on our hearts and say 'I have achieved something really worthwhile this term.'?"

Me and Rosie put our hands on our hearts.

Corridor
9:30 a.m.

Oh bloody marvy. Wet Lindsay, who was stick-insecting around on snitcher duty, saw us with our hands on our hearts and is gave us her world famous 'How childish you are' lecture. Ho hum, pig's bum. Another fabulous opportunity to look at Mrs No Forehead.

9:36 a.m.

Hahahahaha! While Wet Lindsay was telling us off, me and Rosie kept our eyes fixed on her forehead. She couldn't say we were doing anything wrong, but afterwards she scuttled off to the loos for forehead inspection.

The staring campaign continues!

And she doesn't know I am off to America to a Snog Fest with the Luuurve God.

I said to Rosie as we ambled off to the Science block, "He

♥ 27

probably only took her to Late and Live because he is in the European Union for the preservation of rare species."

Rosie said, "What? The 'No Forehead Stick-insect Fighting Fund'?"

"Absolutemento *mon* pally."

We are indeed vair vair *amusant*.

Blodge

Miss Baldwin has got gigantic basoomas. Even bigger than my mutti's, and that is saying something. I was very much afraid that she would set fire to them with the Bunsen burner. Sadly there was no basooma incendiary action, so I couldn't use the foam extinguisher, which would have topped the lesson off in my humble opinion.

On the knicker toaster
Break

I told the Ace Gang about Operation Go to Hamburger-a-gogo Land. They were, as usual, agog as two gogs. Three gogs in Ellen's case. Thank the Lord she seems to have dropped her infectious laugh. I was going to have to kill her if she kept it up.

As we crunched through our nutritious snacks of cheesy Wotsits and chuddie, I said, "It is going to be marv, as I said to Jas – even though she didn't get it – we will be like the Thelma and Louise of England."

Rosie said, "But you won't have a gun."

"I might do."

"No, you won't. Your dad won't let you go to an all-nighter, so he is definitely not going to get you a gun."

"He is. He said I could have one when I got there."

Rosie just looked at me.

"Just a small one for emergency shooting."

They all just looked at me.

Ellen said (annoyingly), "Where... er... where is Masimo? I mean where is he going to be in America?"

I said, "Well, you know, near where we are going to be."

She went on in her vague, dumped-by-Dave-the-Laugh way. "Yes, but I mean, well... where are you going to be?"

I said, "At the clown-car convention in America."

Rosie blew a big gob-stopper bubble and then sucked it back in again. Then she put her face right up close to mine and said slowly, "Yes, but Georgia, where is the clown-car convention?"

♥ 29

"Memphis."

"And where is that?"

I laughed and said, "Good grief, I thought I was bad at geoggers. Don't you know?"

"YOU don't know, do you?"

"Of course I do. It's... down... a... bit from New York."

"Down a bit from New York?"

"Yes."

"Like you thought Hamburg was famous for its hamburgers?"

What had Rosie turned into? Memo the Memory Man? Honestly, just because I had been secretly exfoliating my legs under the desk in geoggers when we were doing the Rhine, and Miss Simpson sprang a surprise question on me...

I changed the subject. "So, what do you think I should pack for my trip?"

Jools said, "Well, not knickers, because they don't wear them there."

I said, "Wow, saucy minxes! You mean they go round in the nuddy-pants? They don't mention that in geoggers, do they? It's all boring stuff about wheat belts and the Atlantic drift."

Jools said, "Panties."

I said, "Oy, clear off with your panties talk. You are a nice-looking girl and everything, but I am just not interested."

Jools said, "No, that's what the Hamburgese wear."

The bell went.

Donner and Blitzen! How am I supposed to discuss my wardrobe if we keep having to go to lessons?

Oh, hang on though, it's German next, so that's OK. We can discuss it then without being disturbed.

German

Herr Kamyer was, as usual, rambling on about the Koch family going on one of their endless camping trips.

Keeping in mind that Koch is pronounced 'cock', and keeping in mind that they are the family that star in our German textbooks, you have to ask yourself this: what sadist decided to feature a family called Koch in our textbooks? They know that they are going to be read out by the naff and the sad (German teachers) to a load of giggling and hysterical girls obsessed with boys and rudey-dudeyness. The family could have been called anything, couldn't they? Schwartz or Schmidt, for instance, but oh no, it had to be the Kochs and their spangleferkels. How many sausages can one family eat? In the Kochs' case, the answer is A LOT.

I put my hand up because I am *sehr* interested in the Kochs.

Herr Kamyer said, "*Ja*, Georgia?"

I said, "Herr Kamyer, did all the Kochs go camping, or was it just the little Kochs and the big Kochs stayed behind? Or was it a mixture of little and big Kochs that came out?"

The whole class was in uproar. Herr Kamyer was, as usual, completely bewildered. He said, "Vat is zo funny about the Kochs? Do you not haf the Kochs in England?"

Happy days.

As we lolloped off I said, "German is such a restful and amusing language, isn't it? Incomprehensible, obviously. As, indeed, are the *lederhosen* that the Germans go yodelling in."

Jas was in Jasland and said, "You think *The Sound of Music* is what Germany is like, don't you? That's why you always rave on about singing nuns and yodelling."

"Well, *The Sound of Music* is, of course, a documentary-style film. You can't argue with facts, and I do know what I'm talking about because Libby has made me watch it twelve times."

"It was set in Austria."

"Yes... and?"

"Last term you said that Germans were obsessed with goats and cheese."

"Yes... and?"

"That was because you had read *Heidi*, and that was set in Switzerland."

"Jas, what in the name of Beelzebub's stamp collection are you going on about?"

"You are crap at geoggers."

Oh, rave on, fringey nitwit. (I didn't say that bit aloud because I am grooming her to be my sidekick on the Road to Romance.)

Still, in the interests of world peace I might be forced to get the old atlas out and look at where Memphis is and so on.

Work work work, I'm so vair tired. And I still have to walk all the way home.

I wonder if Jazzy will give me a piggyback?

4:30 p.m.
No.

5:00 p.m.
I'll be bloody glad when Gordy is allowed out. When I arrived home he had the rubber plant on his head. I've put the stump back in the plant pot and superglued some of the leaves back on. With a bit of luck it will be all right till we go away, and then I can blame it on whatever fool cat-sits for us.

In my bedroom
How can I find out exactly where Masimo is?

Five minutes later
I can't trust Radio Jas to ask Tom to find out where Masimo has gone in Hamburger-a-gogo land. Anytime I ask her anything private it's usually on the Radio Jas airwaves in about two and a half minutes. Her idea of being subtle and finding out things is that she goes out into the street and shouts, "Anyone know anything about this secret thing I am never going to mention?"

Hmmmmmmmmm.

I hate to admit it, but I need the assistance of Dave the Laugh.

Donner and Blitzen!

If I could just accidentally bump into him on the way home then I wouldn't have to phone him.

Ten minutes later

Because if I phone him and Rachel is there I will feel like a facsimile of a sham. I mean he is officially (ish) going out with her.

Five minutes later

Even though he keeps snogging me.

Ten minutes later

Anyway, how can I trust anything he says – it was him, after all, who said he fancied my mum!

But then he is also my mate and official Hornmeister.

Also, he said that I have accidentally done the right thing and become Mystery Girl with Masimo.

Tuesday May 10th
on the way home

Jas and me were ambushed by four Foxwood lads. Two of them deliberately ran into my legs on their bikes, fell off, got back on backwards and started circling us really fast yelling, "You slags!!"

Why?

We were just looking at them and then they fell off their bikes again, this time down a ditch. While they were climbing out we set off walking. After a couple of minutes we noticed they were lurking along behind us, pretending not to follow us. Then Dave the Laugh and his mates appeared round the corner. Dave smiled. He has a great smile and he looked as if he was really glad to see me. He has grown his hair a bit since I last saw him and it looked very cool. Oh shutupshutup, voice of the Horn.

He said, "Hello, Sex Kitty and pal."

Then he saw the boy bloodhounds following us.

"Well, if it isn't Tosser Thompson and his band of trainee tossers. On your way kids."

Dave really is quite well built and he was just standing looking at them.

36

One of the trainee tossers said, "Come on, it's not worth it." and they shuffled off, shoving each other and making pretend farting noises.

Wow! It was a bit like *Gladiator*. But not set in Roman times, and Dave was wearing his school trousers and not a goatskin... More's the pity. Shutupshutup.

Dave put his arm around me.

"You entice them, you know, with your sparkling personality and magnificent nungas."

He is soooo annoying. And rude. I tried to have a strop, but he is notoriously difficult to do that with.

As we walked along Jas said, "S'later" and went off home. Dave's mates all said "S'later" until it was just me and Dave.

I don't know if it's because I'm surpressing my red bottom, but he does seem to be getting better-looking all the time. But no, no, he is not the only one and only. He is yesterday's news. Last week's snog. Anyway, I said to him, "Aren't you rushing to meet your GIRLFRIEND? Won't your GIRLFRIEND be upset if she sees you with me?"

And he started that, "Are you mad?" thing. I managed to stop myself joining in, otherwise it would have developed into tickly bears and then possibly number six. Who knows?

Who knows what goes on in my mind? I will be the last to know. Even when I am totally and without doubtosity in luuurve, absolutely wouldn't dream of being with anyone else, etc. etc., still the Cosmic Horn rears its ugly head. And there is something about Dave and his special lip-nibbling technique. In fact he is one of the best snoggers I have come across, and I haven't even snogged Masimo yet. What if Italian boys are useless in the snoggosity department? What if Masimo looks cool but is a nunga-pouncer like Mark Big Gob? Or kisses all wet and sucky like Whelk Boy?

Dave interrupted my brain, thank the Lord.

"So, how are you, chicklet?

I said, "Fab fanks. I'm going to Hamburger-a-gogo land for a clown-car convention."

Dave looked at me.

"YOU are going to a clown-car convention? Mad as a hen."

I got quite huffy.

"I am very interested in old cars, as you know, and—"

Dave said, "You would rather snog Spotty Norman than go to a clown-car convention."

Fair point well made.

I said, "Well, there is another reason..."

Dave raised one of his eyebrows. Which was quite amusing.

We were passing Luigi's and Dave said, "Come on, let's do coffee, man."

And we went in.

Oh, buggering bums buggering bum. Sitting down at one of the tables were Wet Lindsay and Astonishingly Dim Monica. *Sacré* bloody *bleu*.

Perhaps they were doing reverse stalking.

Wet Lindsay almost threw up when she saw me with Dave. But she covered it quickly and was all dillydollyish with him. He said "Hi" and she batted her eyelashes and flicked her hair. She must have read that book, *How to Make Any Twit Fall in Love with You*. If she tried toffee eyes on Dave, I would have to kill her.

Even though Dave was slightly behind me, she looked straight through me and said to him, "Oh, Dave, it was really groovy at Late and Live, wasn't it? Mas and me had a great time. Did you and Rachel?"

I hate her double with knobs on.

Dave was coolosity personified. "Yeah, it was cool."

And then he deliberately pulled a chair out for me at a table not too near the grotesque twins. As I sat down he said loudly enough for them to hear, "Now then, even though you treat me bad, what would you like, Ms Gorgeous?"

He is soooo nice. I really like the way he is... you know... so nice to me.

Five minutes later

As Lindsay and ADM went out, Lindsay gave Dave what she probably thinks (wrongly) is her attractive smile. She said, "Bye, Dave, maybe see you when Mas gets back." Then she stick-insected out of the door, without leaving a slimy trail on the floor, surprisingly.

I said to Dave, "I hate her, I hate her. She called him 'Mas'. How crap is that?"

Dave looked at me.

"You don't like her, then?"

As we drank our coffee (me trying to avoid the foam moustache fandango) I wanted to ask Dave if he could find out where Masimo was. But I didn't think I could just launch in, so I thought I would ask some limbering-up questions first.

"Dave, you know those boys... well, just before you got there, they ran into my legs on their bikes, then they rode off backwards. Then they called us slags."

Dave said, "Ah, the old running into your legs, riding off backwards and calling you slags thing. Ah hum. Well, it's obvious, isn't it?"

"What is?"

"They fancy you."

"Pardon me?"

"Uh-huh. Clear as daylight."

"But why don't they say 'I fancy you'?"

"Because you might reject them in front of their mates."

"So they think running into my legs on their bikes is better?"

"Yep."

"And calling us slags?"

"Yep."

"And they think that after they've done that, I will say, 'Gosh, yes, I would love to go out with you and be your slag. Once my legs heal up.'"

"Yep."

"But that is mad. Boys are mad."

Dave looked all wise and did his eyebrow thing again.

We slurped a bit more, then I said, "But, why? How does it work? You know at break at school, when you talk about personal stuff, well..."

Dave said, "Let me interrupt you there, Kittykat. Lads don't talk about 'stuff' at break. They play footie or that other well-known game, 'Do you know any good dentists?'"

I said, "What?"

"You know: 'Do you know any good dentists? Because you're going to need one in a minute when I have to deck you.'"

Blimey.

Dave went on. "Of course, lads have the same feelings, we just communicate in a different way. Sometimes it does get personal though."

I looked at him. This was better.

"Yeah, for instance, yesterday one of the fifth form hung his girlfriend's knickers out of the science-block window."

5:30 p.m.
Walked home after my session with the Hornmeister still in a bit of a daze. When we said s'later, he gave me a kiss

on the cheek and didn't attempt tickly bears or anything. Perhaps he is going straight. Who knows? But, on the plus side, he has said he'll find out all he can about Masimo for me. He is such a good boy-type pal. He didn't mention Rachel, which is a bit odd as she's supposed to be his girlfriend.

5:35 p.m.

Crossing the High Street I bumped into Tom. I like Tom, even though I think he's mad to go to Kiwi-a-gogo land. And go out with Jas. And go on camping fiascos. And go on about food produce. Other than that, I like him.

He seemed to have a touch of sadnosity about him when he said, "All right, Gee?"

"Yes, fanks all right as an... all-right thing. And you?"

He was unusually silent for him and eventually just said, "You'll look after Jas for me, won't you?"

I said, "You bet your goddamn bottom dollar, mister. I've got a gun and I'm not afraid to use it."

He just looked at me. Like I was talking complete rubbish or something.

6:00 p.m.

Home in my room, covered in unguents for tip-top beautosity.

I will say this: mashed banana is vair vair good for the luuurve complexion, which is not easy to say when you have a face full of mashed banana.

I wish I had a photo of Masimo. I hope I don't forget what he looks like. I'll just lie down in my (unusually empty) bed and have a mental snog with him.

6:25 p.m.

Oh, buggering God's bum. Angus and Gordy have come in and started playing the mouse-disguised-as-a-foot game. They attack my feet for a bit really viciously until I pull my feet up under my bum, then they lie down and go to sleep. But they are not really asleep, they are just doing pretend asleep. As soon as I snuggle down to snooze off into Masimo land, they leap on my foot underneath the blankets and wrestle it. Then they "go to sleep" again. They don't really think my foot is a mouse and that it will creep out when it sees they are asleep, do they?

6:40 p.m.

How did Ms Furry Tart, aka Naomi, get past the armed warden (Vati) and into my bed?

Blimey, I am quite literally lying in a cat basket.

6:45 p.m.

I wish she wouldn't do that lying-on-her-back-with-her-legs-spread-open thing on my bed.

6:50 p.m.

Gordy is sniffing her bottom. This is disgusting!! In front of his dad. This is kitty-porn – surely there must be some sort of helpline for this. A kittykat helpline.

It could be called Paws for Thought.

7:30 p.m.

Oh, Masimo, soon we will be together and you can tell me all about Pizza-a-gogo land. The music. The art. The snogging. I wonder if they have special techniques that go with their passionate Latin temperament? I hope he doesn't get carried away and nibble my lips off.

♥ 45

7:35 p.m.
No, I hope he does! Nibble away, Luuurve God!!

Wednesday May 11th
In my bedroom
7:07 p.m.
How many hours is it till we go to Hamburger-a-gogo? Jas will know. I'm not phoning her though.

Doorbell rang.

I went quietly to the top of the stairs and looked down. Crikey! Loon Alert! It was my grandad, and he was wearing shorts! Not his huge, all-encompassing grandad shorts that he wore during the Boer War, but cycling shorts. In Lycra. Good grief.

Please, please tell me he has not taken up cycling. Please.

I went back to my room quietly.

Maybe if I hide behind the door they will think I am out and JUST GO AWAY.

One minute later
Oh, yeah. Dream on.

Mutti called up, "Georgie, Grandad's here!"

I kept silent behind the door. Naomi, Angus and Gordy were all in my bed – again – doing their idiot-cat-staring-at-me thing. They had better not give my position away. It would be all right if it was just Gordon – then I might have a one in two chance of not being caught; because although one of his eyes is fixed on me, the other is glancing out the window.

The advance loon party came clanking up the stairs.

"Gingey, Gingey, it's meeeeeeee, Libbbbeeeeee... Where is you?"

I heard her huffing and puffing outside my door and doing her alarming laugh. "Hoggyhoggy. Here I come, reggy or nut."

Then she kicked my door and it burst open, very nearly flattening my nose.

"Owwwwww."

She put her mad little face around the door and smiled at me. When, and how, did she lose her front teeth? And why did she think it was attractive to push her tongue through the gap?

"Gingey, there you is! Cheeky monkey."

She threw all the cats off the bed and started tucking

scuba-diving Barbie and Jesus/Sandra up nice and comfy under the duvet. I tried to reason with her.

"Bibsy, that's not really Barbie and... er... Sandra's bed, is it? It's my bed, and there's no room for—"

She put her arms up to me and said, "Kiss."

Oh, blimey. She is cute, though. I picked her up to give her a little cuddle, and she put her hand on my nose and was sort of squeezing it and twirling it around. It was quite painful, actually. Dear God I hope it doesn't swell up.

Grandad was the next to arrive at the open-bedroom loon party.

He popped his head around the door and said, "Hello, love, I've just been to the doctor because I've got a steering wheel down my shorts. I said to him, 'Doctor, will you do something about this steering wheel down my shorts? It's driving me nuts!' Do you see? 'Steering wheel, driving me nuts!' Do you get it? Do you?"

How DISGUSTING!!

He's an octogenarian.

My ears feel like prostitutes.

8:00 p.m.

Thank the Lord, Grandad has gone. Unfortunately not before giving me a present from his "girlfriend" Maisie. I am sorry I ever suggested that Grandad was mad. His girlfriend has reached new and giddy heights of bonkerosity. Have you ever been given knitted toeless socks? In green, yellow and purple?

No, I thought not.

Grandad is going to house-sit the kittykats for the week we are away.

I said to Mutti, "Let's just burn the house to the ground before we go. Because that's what it will be like when we get back. Face it."

Mum said, "You are so rude, Georgia. You'll be old one day yourself."

I was going to go put my toeless socks on to give her the gist of what I was saying about the elderly insane, but then I realised I was on a charm mission. Also, Jas's parents were coming round in half an hour. So I said, "Shall I make some snacks for when Jas's M and D come round?"

She looked at me as if I had turned into a talking egg.

♥

Even Gordy stopped eating Mum's mules and looked at me with one eye.

9:30 p.m.
Phew. Jas and I did secret thumbsie-upsies as she and her mutti and vati left. Yessssss! And thrice yesss! We are off to Hamburger-a-gogo land!!

Jas has got one hundred squids for spendies.

How far can Memphis be from where Masimo is? Wherever that is.

11:00 p.m.
All's well that ends well. Libby is in her own bed with Barbie and Our Lord Sandra, and the big cats have been thrown outside to lay waste to the vole population. Gordy is in his basket in the kitchen. So I can get some well-earned beauty sleep. My nose doesn't seem any more swollen than normal.

11:15 p.m.
Dad says that Elvis Presley lived in Memphis and he was a musician (not that you would know that from the crap songs

that Dad sings). Anyway, he was a musician and Masimo is a musician, ergo Memphis must be somewhere that musicians hang out.

Midnight

Pray God that Dad doesn't take his Elvis Presley quiff with him. Sometimes for a "joke" he sticks the quiff on and starts shaking his hips about. It's disgusting – and also probably very dangerous hipwise for a man of his years.

He and his lardy mates, the "lads" think it's hilarious.

It isn't.

12:05 a.m.

Anyway, what do I care, I am on Cloud Nine in Luuurve Heaven.

We go on 22nd May, which is eleven days away. I am sooooo excited.

12:10 a.m.

Hawkeye called me a ninny and said that I "had the attention span of a pea" but what she doesn't know is that I have powers of discipline that would surprise a lot of people

♥ 51

who accuse me of laziosity. When I put my mind to it I can do stuff. For instance, even though I'm tired now and it's midnight, it is imperative that I get up and go to the bathroom and cleanse and tone my... zzzzzz zzzzzzzzzzzzz.

Thursday May 12th
Ten days to Hamburger-a-gogo land
On the way to school

"Jas, I am so vair vair full to the brim with excitementosity. Aren't you?"

"Hmmm."

"Yes, so am I. Let's sing 'New York, New York' to get us in the mood."

"No."

"That's the spirit. You see, that is why coming to Hamburger-a-gogo is sooo good for you – it will broaden what there is of your mind."

I started to sing, "I want to be a part of it, New York, New YORK!!!!!"

I stopped because of intense pensioner-glaring when we passed the post office.

Jas was slouching along by my side like a trusty... badger.

"Jas, why do they call it that? New York, New York? We don't say London, London, do we?"

"Hmmmm."

"Perhaps it's because Hamburgese people are a bit on the slow side and don't get it immediately, so they have to say it twice."

9:30 p.m.

Vati made us watch a really old film tonight with John Wayne in it.

Midnight

I was right to be worried about them being a bit on the slow side. Crikey, John Waaaaaaayne speaks slowly. If all Americans speak so slowly, I'll be there all day queueing up behind people as they ask for a cup of "caaaaaawwwwwfffeeeee". (And I won't even know why I am in the queue, as I don't even like caawwfffee.)

Also, if Dad doesn't stop singing Elvis songs I may go insane.

Friday May 13th

Nine days to Hamburger-a-gogo land

Dawn

Dad burst into my room in his pyjamas and Elvis quiff, singing "Heartbreak Hotel".

Still, now that I'm up, I'll make a list of stuff to take to Hamburger-a-gogo.

7:25 a.m.

This is my packing list:

1. Make-up essentials
2. Really gorgey clothes

I've gathered my make-up essentials together and they fill a suitcase.

I wonder if I can get Jazzy to put some of my make-up in her bag. Mind you, knowing her, she's already filled her bag with her ginormous knickers – or big "panties", as we must learn to call them now.

Although "big panties" reminds me of incontinent knickers.

Still, let the Americans have it their way. I love them all. And I mean that most sincerely. Even though I have never met them.

Chaos headquarters

Mutti was dragging Gordy out of Libby's rucksack, and Libby was hitting Mum on the head with her spoon.

"Bad Mummy, bad."

Libby had hidden Gordy in her rucky because she wanted to take him to nursery school with her. But even Mum noticed the rucksack walking around by itself.

Then the phone rang.

Mutti yelled at me, "Get that, Georgia, it's bound to be one of your daft friends."

Oh, that is nice, isn't it? It's much more likely to be one of her daft friends.

I answered it and said, "Yes, hello. Reception speaking, Hotel Insane."

It was Dave the Laugh. Oh my giddy God, and I hadn't even got any lip gloss on.

He said, "Hi, Sex Kitty, Hornmeister here. I'm in a hurry, but thought you would like to know that the extremely flash Masimo, who I personally feel might be on the gay side handbagwise—"

"Dave..."

♡ 55

"OK, OK. All I can find out is that he is staying in Manhattan and his surname is Scarlotti."

I said, "Oh, thank you thank you, Dave."

"It's cool. I'm sure we can think of some way you can repay me – it may involve heavy snogging. Bye."

And he put the phone down.

Yipppppeeeee!!!

Manhattan, here I come!

8:30 a.m.

Ran to meet Jas.

She was all flustered like a fringey loon.

I said, "Howdy."

"Come on, Georgia, we'll be late."

As we galloped along, I said, "I am going to speak American all day today."

Jas went, pant pant, "They speak English."

I said, "Don't be mad," pant pant.

We arrived on time, but only just. Wet Lindsay was on sadist duty. She looked at us as we panted by her like we were a couple of turds in uniform.

"Can't you two grow up and be on time for once?"

I gave her a big smile while gazing at her ear, and said, "Howdy. Now you all have a nice day. You hear?"

She stomped off to terrorise some first formers, but she was fingering her lugholes. Hahahahahaha. And also *hasta la vista*, baby.

Maths

God, maths is boring. And complete bollocks.

When I marry Masimo, I will have manservants to do my adding up for me.

And my quadratic equations, which I will never use.

Lunchtime

Operation Track Down the Luuurve God

Made Jas come to the library with me.

Miss Wilson almost fell off her stool when we came in.

I calmed her by saying, "Alrighty? Now you all have a nice day."

We lugged the big atlas to a table, and I leafed through the maps until I got to America and found New York, New York.

I said to Jas, "Now, where is Memphis, Memphis?"

Jas found it and said, "It looks a bit far down."

For once she is not wrong. On the plus side, Manhattan is only about an eighth of an inch long.

But it is about two feet from Memphis.

Still, there must be buses. Surely?

4:30 p.m.

On the way home I was singing "Home, home on the range, where the deer and the antelope play" to Jazzy. She loves a bit of a singsong.

I said that. I said, "You love a bit of a singsong, don't you, Jazzy?"

"No."

"See, I knew you did. You do a little dance while I sing the chorus. You could do a dance based on a deer. Go on, do the little deer dance, make your feet like—"

And that is when she kicked me. She can be very violent.

She said, "I haven't told him yet."

"What? Who?"

"Hunk— er, I mean Tom, about Hamburger-a-gogo land."

I looked at her in amazednosity. Radio Jas, the voice of the nation, had not told Hunky something?

She said, "I can be just as independent and adventurous as him."

I didn't laugh, even though I have seen the amount of knickers that Jas thinks she will need for seven days.

I MUST sort out my clothes this weekend.

Le Weekend

11:00 a.m.

Now then, I am going to take a "capsule" wardrobe. It's what Naomi Campbell and all the top models do. They just take the absolute essentials with them when they travel.

12:00 p.m.

I'm exhausted, but I have managed to whittle my capsule wardrobe down to six cases.

12:01 p.m.

And a rucksack.

12:03 p.m.

Apart from my shoes, which I can't get in, but Mum will probably put them in her case.

12:30 p.m.

Nobody has yet told Libby that Angus and Gordy are not coming with us on our holidays.

12:35 p.m.

When someone does tell her, I'll tell you one thing for free – it will not be me. I need all my limbs for my Luuurve Quest.

12:40 p.m.

Libby has made Gordy a paper bikini for his holidays, which might come in handy if he were coming on holiday.

And cats wore bikinis.

And if he hadn't immediately destroyed it and then buried it in the rubber plant.

Sunday May 15th
Seven days to Hamburger-a-gogo land
Midday

I hate my dad. He is so unreasonable. It's like dealing with a spoiled child.

I asked Mum if she would be so kind as to slip my shoes in her case, and all hell broke loose.

Dad said, "Why don't you put them in your case?"

And I said, "Because, Father, all of my cases are full."

Vati came stropping into my bedroom, saw my cases, and said, "Don't be ridiculous! You can take one case. That is it."

I said, "Excuse me if I'm right, Dad, but do you want me to look like a poor person in front of the Hamburgese? I am representing the English nation abroad."

But you might as well be talking to yourself.

2:00 p.m.

I've repacked, but there are still three cases of essentials. *Sacré* bloody *bleu*.

Jas phoned to tell me that she told Hunky about her trip and he has had the boy version of a nervy spaz. He phoned her eighteen times in two hours.

"He was so upset."

"Yes, you said."

"Really really upset. He phoned me eighteen times in two hours."

"Er... I know."

"Eighteen times."

"Wow... How many times did you say he phoned?"

I said it ironically, but Jas didn't get it. She just went on and on. "Eighteen times, and then he came round this morning really early and posted a love-poem-song-type thing through my door."

Oh no. Not a love poem.

"Do you want to hear it?"

"No."

"It's called, 'You are the only fish in my sea'.

Good Lord. Tom's whole family is obsessed with livestock.

To cheer her up and to get me out of my packing nightmare scenario I called a gang meeting.

The park, sitting on the swings
4:30 p.m.

Jas has read her poem to everyone, so I hope she's got it out of her system now. It is truly crap. That is a fact. But I didn't say so; I wanted Jas to perk up for our big adventure. I was soooo excited, and I was standing up swinging on a swing, singing "I want to be in America! Everything's free in America!!!"

Then Ellen said, "Georgia, have you actually snogged Masimo yet?"

I laughed in a sultry way. "Have I snogged Masimo? Have I—"

Jas said, "No, she hasn't. Well, not unless you count two seconds, which I don't, and anyway it's not on the snogging scale, so it's not... on the... snogging scale."

Oh, thanks, bestest pally NOT. I wish I had told her what I thought about Fish Boy's poem now.

Jools said, "Do you think Wet Lindsay has snogged him? You know, when they went to Late and Live. She must have, you know... wanted to."

Ohhhnooo. Get out of my head.

I said, "Who in their right mind would snog Wet Lindsay?"

Jools said, "Well, actually, Robbie must have snogged her because they went out together and—"

I started humming in my head so I didn't have to listen to this; it was making me feel quite sick.

Jas said, "Perhaps some kinds of boys like tiny foreheads. Tom said that he knows a boy who's mad for girls who wear really thick glasses."

Good grief. Still, at least, there was a chance for Nauseating P. Green.

Ellen was obviously in her own dream world. "That mate of Tom's – Speedy – asked me out when I was down the square, but... oh... I don't know, it's just there is something. I mean, he's nice but I still... you know... have feelings for... well, you know... Do you think?"

I said, "Can I ask you something, Ellen? What are you raving on about?"

I wished I hadn't asked.

"I mean Dave the Laugh. Is he going out with Rachel still... or ... er... what?"

Jas said, "He wasn't with her when we saw him the other day, was he, Gee? Did he mention her when you went for a coffee?"

Oh shutupshutup about Dave the sodding Laugh.

Ellen was just about to start the "I didn't know that you saw Dave the Laugh, what did you talk about, did he mention me, how come you went for a coffee with him?" scenario when Mabs saved my bacon (ish).

She said, "How do you know that Masimo wants to see you?"

"Well, he asked me for my telephone number and I couldn't give it to him because my head was about to drop off from redness. So he said, "OK, Miss Hard to Get, I will see you later, when I get back from America."

Ellen was looking at me. "So he said 'See you later' then?"

I said, "No, not just 'see you later' like in 's'later' but more—"

But Ellen was locked into her own ramblosity. "Dave the Laugh said 'see you later' to me and I did the flicky hair and everything and dancing by myself and so on... and then he went off with Rachel."

The gang started nodding wisely (not).

I said, "Yes, but Masimo said 'see you later' after I had become Mystery Woman."

Rosie said, "Mystery Woman?"

"Yes, after I had accidentally treated him to my glaciosity."

Rosie had her face really close to mine.

"You are Mystery Woman?"

All the gang looked at me.

Jools said, "You are MYSTERY Woman?"

Then Mabs said, "YOU are Mystery Woman?"

What is this, a parrots' convention?

Rosie said, "Mystery Woman. You are Mystery Woman.

Not as you used to be – 'Oooooooh my boy entrancers have stuck together' Woman?"

Home
5:30 p.m.
Oh boo. Now I've got the screaming heebie-jeebies and doubtosity all rolled into one. Perhaps Masimo says "See you when I get back, Miss Hard to Get" to everyone.

5:45 p.m.
Just when you think things couldn't get any worse, they take a turn for the worserer.

Grandad has cancelled his cat duties because he's going on a bicycling tour to the Lake District. He says he has heard the call of the wild and is setting out tonight with his backpack.

I cannot believe the utter selfishosity of the elderly.

5:50 p.m.
Family "conference" (aka Dad shouting a lot).

We can't think of anyone stupid... er... kind enough to look after Angus and Gordy.

6:15 p.m.

Mum has tried all her so-called aerobics friends and none of them will come over.

I said to her, "Did you tell them about the mice cream incident?"

Of course she has, so she has only herself to blame.

6:30 p.m.

Sadly I have also shown off about Angus and Gordy's "adventures" and alluring little habits *vis à vis* woodland animals, pooing, etc. So none of my friends will have anything to do with them. Rosie said that Sven said he'd look after Angus and Gordy in a cave he has found. But the whole idea of that is far, far too weird.

Vati said, "What about a cattery, then?"

That's when Angus came in with a spade. We all just looked at one another.

Vati said, "Well, there is only one thing for it. I'm going to have to ask for a bit of neighbourly support."

7:15 p.m.

Dad went to Mr Next Door first. As he went through the

♡ 67

door he said, "Alfred and I have always had a bit of an understanding, although I know we've had our differences *vis à vis* the damage Angus has done to his rhododendrons—"

I said, "And when he rounded the Prat Poodles up and trapped them in the greenhouse."

"Yes, well..."

"And then rode them round like little horsies."

"Yes, well..."

"And the dog psychiatrist having to come in."

Dad took his coat off.

7:25 p.m.

Dad said, "I'll just pop across the road to Colin and, you know, see if maybe he could just keep an eye on feeding them."

7:28 p.m.

Dad's back.

He said, "He laughed."

Dad has slammed off to the pub to talk to Uncle Eddie and see if he knows any fools who might help us out.

Doorbell rang. I looked down the stairs from the safety of my bedroom.

Mutti answered. Uh-oh. It was one of our beloved boys in blue. And as policemen go, he didn't look pleased. Now what?

I scampered down the stairs to give my mutti moral support. Although, as it happens, basooma support would have been more appropriate. Hasn't she got one single piece of clothing that doesn't reveal far too much flesh?

I put an interested look on my face. It's the one I use when Hawkeye asks me where my homework is. It usually results in double detention, but you can't have everything. The constable looked at me, and it wasn't his guardian-of-the-community-and-servant-of-the-people look.

He said to Mum, "Good evening, madam, can you tell me if you know this person?" And he held up Grandad's O.A.P. card, the one with the photo of him with the earring in.

Don't ask.

Mum said, "Yes, it's my father... Oh My God, is he all right?"

The officer said, "Yes, he is, madam, but he is a danger to himself and others."

I said, "You can say that again, officer. I don't need a helmet and truncheon to figure that out."

Mum said, "Shut up, Georgia."

Which I think is probably abusive behaviour, but I let it go.

It turns out that, for once, the officer was the bearer of glad tidings. Grandad had set out on his six-hundred-mile bike ride to the Lake District and fell off at the end of his street. But not before he knocked the policeman off his new community bike.

"I'd only had it for a week, madam."

I tried to look concerned.

The policeman opened his notebook. "The gentleman we have now positively identified as your father was wearing Lycra shorts and kept falling off his bike. I asked him to walk a straight line."

Mutti said, "Oh my goodness, had he been drinking?"

The officer said, "I don't know, madam, but he refused to walk the line on account of an old war wound. Then he said..." The officer looked down at his notes again. "...'Do you want to come back to my place, constable, and have one for the road?'"

You have to give Grandad full marks on the lunacy scale.

8:00 p.m.

The policeman radioed into his station and Grandad was released from chokey after being charged with careless biking and not having a bell. Apparently the budgie bell he had Sellotaped on to the handlebar doesn't count.

He now has a criminal record.

Mum was all flustered and kept apologising to the policeman as he went off. "I am so sorry, officer. I hope you can mend your bike and you haven't been hurt at all."

The policeman said, "No, well, I'm quite tough, madam."

"Yes, well you do seem very fit. I do a bit of aerobics myself; it's awfully good for keeping in shape."

The policeman winked at her (honestly!) and he said, "Yes, I can see that. Anyway, madam, I'd better be on my way."

And then he said that classic thing that you think you'd only see on TV. He said, "Mind how you go, it's a jungle out there."

Mum practically wet herself with laughing. She is so so

sad and embarrassing. After the policeman had gone I just looked at her, and she said, "What? What?"

I said, "You know what. You were practically slavering over him."

"Well, he was a nice young man – of course, far too young for me."

Unbelievable!!!

In my bedroom
How very embarrassing my family is.

Midnight
Still, on the plus side, Grandad's cycling days are over and he can now be on house-burning-down duties for when we go to Hamburger-a-gogo land. Hurrah! And also zippety doo dah!!

Tuesday May 17th
Five days to Hamburger-a-gogo land
Evening
Oh, I just can't stand this hanging around waiting to go on the Luuurve Plane.

Come on come on!!!

I've been trying out arrival outfits. Boots or shoes? It's hard to know what to do weatherwise. Also, I may have to go from day wear to evening wear, depending on the time-zone business.

I am practising speaking Hamburgese, even in my own head. The key seems to be to add stuff, so instead of weather you say weatherwise. Timewise. Daywise. Luuurvewise, etc.

But on a more seriouswise note, this time business is v.v. aggravating fashionwise.

I said to Jas on the phone (she is opting for sensible sports casual for travelling)... I said to her (Mistress of the Time Lords), "Are we flying backwards in time, or what?"

"Yeah, they are six hours behind us."

"Why are they? Why can't they just keep up with us? Didn't we invent time?"

"What?"

"You know, Greenwich Mean Time – didn't we invent it? So why can't they just be the same as us?"

"Because they would be getting up in the middle of the night."

"So?"

But you can't reason with Jas.

Wednesday May 18th
Four days to Hamburger-a-gogo land
Evening

Grandad has come round for instructions about looking after the house and cats.

I am still in a ditherspaz about what to wear. I've been through all of my clothes about a million times.

Still, on the plus side, I have definitely decided what to wear nailwise. I've chosen Pouting Pink.

I am absolutely full of exhaustiosity.

8:15 p.m.

Dragged myself downstairs for a reviving snack.

In the front room

Grandad started fiddling about in his pockets.

"I've got something for you."

Oh, joy unbounded. A boiled sweet.

I love him and everything, but why does he have to

be so, you know... so... grandadish?

The TV was on, with my extremely unfit vati lolling around in front of it. As I sat down to try and get my tights away from Gordy, Vati said, "Now then, Georgia, why don't you tell me how much spending money you expect for the holiday. Then we'll have a good laugh and go from there."

Vair vair amusing. Sadly though, I have to humour him. I said, "Well, it's only for a week, isn't it? And we've got the hotel rooms and food and so on, so actually, all in all, I think a thousand quid would just about cover it if I don't buy anything extravagant."

Mum said, "Don't be silly, Georgia."

Grandad said, "Do you remember when you took Georgia to the doctor's surgery when she was a couple of weeks old?"

Mum ruffled my hair (very annoying) and looked all nostalgic. "I remember every single thing about your life, darling girl. You've been a pleasure and joy to me from the moment you were born."

Dad said, "Bloody hell, Connie! Calm down."

But Mum had gone off into Mumland, "Do you know

you had no hair when you were born – all baldy, like Uncle Eddie. So sweet."

Oh God.

Grandad was still rambling on like Rambling Sid Rumpo. "Yes, and there was that woman in the waiting room."

Mum went, "Oooh, yes, I'd forgotten her."

Grandad said, "And she was looking in all the prams and going 'oooh what a lovely baby' and then she looked in at Georgia and said 'Christ look at the conk on this baldy one! Come and look!'"

What?

All the 'grown-ups' were laughing.

Mum said, "Well that's why I always used to stroke your nose every time I fed you, so that I could sort of squeeze it into shape a bit."

I left the room and went into the hall. I looked in the mirror. My nose had been fondled from birth and it was still like it was?

Phoned Jas, "Jas, do you think I have grown into my nose?"

Jas went, "Hahahahahha... er... yes."

"But do you think it's still quite big?"

Jas was chewing something. "Well, let's put it this way... it's a generous nose."

10:00 p.m.
Generous.

2:00 a.m.
Woke up from a dream where a customs official at the airport charged me excess baggage for my nose.

Thursday May 19th
Three days to Hamburger-a-gogo land
In bed
11:00 p.m.
I am sleeping on my back and I've made a sort of splint for my nose out of elastoplasts and matchsticks, so at least it can't grow any more.

Friday May 20th
Two days to Hamburger-a-gogo land
8:00 a.m.
Tore off the elastoplasts. Ow bugger and ow and buggery

ow! I hope Masimo appreciates what a lot of trouble I'm going to beautywise, although unless my brain drops out, I will not be telling him that I sleep in a nose splint.

Went down to the kitchen for brekky. Yip yip and three times yip, in fact yipyipyip!! Last day at Stalag 14 and then I set off on the *grand* adventure *de* LUUURVE.

Bathroom
8:10 a.m.
I've been keeping up a daily plucking plan to keep the orang-utan gene at bay. However, I may get Jas to do an impartial inspection of the backs of my legs, as it's useless being smoothy smooth on the front if you're chimpish at the back.

Lalala. Massage in exfoliating products (Mum's) and make small circles to slough off naughty old cells and leave skin like baby's botty (without the poo).

The flight is eight hours, so I should have just about enough time to apply my make-up, do my nails and then be ready to bump into Masimo in a casual and natural way.

Lunchtime

As it is raining quite hard, for once we're allowed to loll around in the canteen. Sadly that means we have spectacular sad sacks as company. The rest of the Ace Gang went to the loo to redo their hair – they are so vain, they're like a bunch of Chelsea footballers. I bagsied a table by putting all my things on five chairs and then pretended to be learning my part as Macduff in *MacUseless* just in case Nauseating P. Green saw me by myself and came to tell me about her hamsters. Or her new enormous glasses. Her being cast as Lady Macduff is the worst thing that has happened. I think she thinks we are actually man and wife.

I was so busy pretending to read that I didn't notice the whiff of tiny foreheadedness until it was too late. I looked up to see Wet Lindsay sitting down with her skungy mates at the table next to me.

She said, "Georgia, normal people only need one chair to sit on. Clear those bags up."

I looked at her, and I was going to say something like, "Normal people have a bit of skull between their eyebrows and their fringe," but she was quite likely to give me detention, even on the last day of term. So I let a small smile play around my lips and imagined her in her thong crashing into the sanitary towel dispenser, like she did last term. Happy memories.

As I didn't respond, she went back to talking absolute bollocks to her sad mates. I don't know what was keeping the Ace Gang, unless Ellen had had another dither attack and fallen down in the lavatory. Or maybe Jas was chatting about her fringe.

I was unwrapping my lunchtime Jammy Dodger when I nearly fell off my chair. I could hear Lindsay whining on, whiney whine, and then she said, "Mas is having a great time in the States, he's been gigging with a group in New York an—"

What? What??

I was interrupted by the gang arriving. They were all singing "My gosh I'm fit, but don't I know it!" so loudly that I couldn't hear anything else Wet Lindsay said.

On the way home
4:30 p.m.
"Jas, HOW could he be in touch with her? Did he phone her? Why? Why?"

80

"Well, I don't know, but he's not... he's not, like, your boyfriend, is he? And..."

"Jas, I hope you are not going to try and be reasonable, because then I really will have to kill you."

Bedroom

Oh, no. I am once more on the rack of love.

I must speak to the Hornmeister.

Even if I show no pridenosity, I must know what he thinks.

I can't phone him now, though, in front of Mum. Why can't I have a mobile phone?

Oh Goddy God God.

5:00 p.m.

Libby has got her "boyfwen" Josh with her. Even my little sister has got a boyfriend. She and Joshy went off into her room and I could hear them murmuring and singing together.

Oh, I am so fed up.

5:15 p.m.

Mum is still pratting about; for once when I wish she was out she is in. Typico. She said, "Why are you mooning around? What are you up to?"

Honestly.

5:20 p.m.

I can't bear this tensionosity.

Libby came into my room to sing me a new song that she learned at nursery. I noticed that Josh had quite a lot of lipstick on. She cleared her throat and then began singing in her little but very piercing voice. The tune is the same one as for "Sex Bum". Quite quite delightful.

She sang, "Bum oley, bum oley, arsey arsey bum bum. Poo poo and bummy bum bum arse!!"

Yes, that is what my little sister is learning at her nursery school.

Songs about bottoms.

5:30 p.m.

I must speak to Dave.

Libby's back in for another round of "Sex Bum".

Oh good, Josh knows the words, too.

6:00 p.m.
Mum had to quickly scrub Josh so that his mummy will let him play with Libby again. I don't think Josh's mum suspected anything when she collected him. But she hasn't heard his lovely song yet.

7:00 p.m.
I HAVE to speak to Dave.

Crept downstairs, Mutti and Vati and Uncle Eddie are in the front room discussing the clown-car convention. When I listened at the door, I could hear them raving on.

Vati was saying, "Apparently there's a Robin Reliant from the sixties that has its original wheel hubs."

And Uncle Eddie said, "I've packed my special comedy underpants."

Good grief.

I girded up my loins and dialled Dave's number. What if he was with Rachel? That would be the *coup de* poo.

Oh, it was ringing. Maybe... I should just... Then he answered the phone.

"Dave?"

"*Bonsoir*, it is he."

"I must ask you something."

"Is that you, Georgia? I'm afraid I never do phone sex; I think it cheapens things."

"Dave, please..."

Later

Feel a bit better. Dave can be really nice in an annoying way. He's off to a club night tonight and Dom from the Stiff Dylans will be there, so he's going to find out what he can about Masimo and Wet Lindsay.

In my bedroom of pain
9:30 p.m.

Why can't my life be simple?

And happy.

Tell me that, Jesus.

I have rescued Jesus from Libby and replaced him on my dressing table. I've taken off the frock that Libby put on, but I can't get the rouge off. He looks like he has a bit of a holiday tan.

When was the last time I had fun?

Never, that's when.

I don't think I will ever laugh again.

In bed looking at the moon
11:00 p.m.

I wonder if Masimo is looking at the same moon as I am. He's probably too busy thinking about Wet Lindsay to look at the moon.

I read one of the many many books that Mum buys to try and make herself a better person – I think it was called "I'm OK, you're OK, but what if we only think we're OK but we're not really OK." – anyway, whatever it was called, it said in the book that men like blonde girls with sort of baby faces because they think they are babies and want to look after them.

Have I got a baby face?

Looking in the mirror.

Even when I was officially a baby and I did have a baby face, you wouldn't have known because my nose covered most of it.

I pushed the tip of it back with my finger.

Would boys like me better if I looked like a small pig with a bob?

Who knows?

Who cares?

I'm not even going to bother putting my nose splint on.

11:20 p.m.

The fact is that Wet Lindsay has heard from Masimo and I haven't.

And not one single person on the planet cares. That is the point, really – who does care? If I just disappeared from the planet, who would really care?

11:25 p.m.

I bet if I committed suicide no one would notice for days. And then, when I did get found, they'd all be going, "Why did she do such a stupid thing? She was always so happy and cheerful and brave. She never complained."

They would never suspect the deep sadnosity that had tainted my life.

11:30 p.m.

They might if I wrote a note spelling it out even for the very very dim.

I got a piece of paper and started a suicide note.

Dear Mum and Dad,

I can't go on any longer. Some people just cannot see beyond the superficial.

Maybe noses shouldn't count, but they do. It is tragic that you cannot pick your own nose. (Hang on a minute, that sounds a bit wrong, I'll cross that out.) People may say I am a crazy mixed-up confused teenager. Maybe they are right. Maybe they are wrong.

Who are they, anyway?

I realise I am an embarrassment to you all. Grandad in particular has said this many times. But the fact is I am too sensitive for this life.

Goodbye. I love you all.

Georgia

p.s. Don't blame yourself, Dad. You have learned to live with your nose. I can't.

I could imagine them all at my funeral. People crying,

looking at the photos I had enclosed in the suicide-note envelope. In particular, that really nice one that Jas took of me in my groovy leather skirt and boots. My mum gazing at the photo and crying and saying, "But she was BEAUTIFUL. So beautiful. Why didn't she realise it?" A woman coming up and saying, "I am from a modelling agency. Why, oh why did no one tell me about this girl? She is the most photogenic girl I have come across in all my long years of talent hunting." Them gazing at me in my coffin and crying... as they tried to force the coffin lid down over my nose!

Merde.

Saturday May 21st
One day to Hamburger-a-gogo land
9:30 a.m.

Re-reading my suicide note. I could kill myself now so as not to waste the note.

I can't really be bothered, though. I'd have to get out of bed.

What is the point of going to Hamburger-a-gogo land, or even *thinking* about Masimo, if he isn't interested in me and likes Old Thongy?

Anyway, what could I commit suicide with? There aren't any pills lying around the place because Mum and Dad are just too cheerful to bother getting any. And I'm not trying anything else, because it might hurt.

10:30 a.m.
Anyway, there's so much noise coming from the bathroom, how I am supposed to concentrate on being depressed?

Vati is giving Angus a bath in preparation for our holidays. I can hear him yelling, "Right, that's it, it's no use struggling. Angus, my friend, you are going in that bath for a good scrub. You smell like a dustbin."

The phone rang, but no one answered it, of course, so I dragged myself downstairs.

It was Dave. Ohmygiddygod.

He said, "OK, this is the deal."

At which point there was an enormous splash from the bathroom and my vati started shouting and swearing like the lunatic he is. "Buggering bastard bollocking bloody... SHIIIITE!!!"

Dave said, "What in the name of arse is going on?"

I was just about to apologise for my father, when

♥ 89

he appeared at the bathroom door absolutely soaking. He had obviously fallen in the bath.

He looked at me and said, "Don't say a bloody word."

It was vair and thrice times vair *amusant*. I didn't laugh, though, because a) I might be heartbroken, and b) if I'm not, I might still want to go to Hamburger-a-gogo.

I whispered to Dave, "My vati has just been bathing Angus with a firm hand, but sadly he has fallen in the bath himself."

Dave said, "I love your house. Anyway, this is the deal: Masimo, the well-known Italian homosexualist—"

"Dave..."

"Anyway, he sent a postcard to Dom and a couple to the other lads in the Stiff Dylans, and they all seem to have the same theme – you know, like, 'I am a flash Italian git on my holidays' type scenarios. Dom told Lindsay about the gigging in New York and so on. In my Hornmeister opinion, you are in exactly the same position as you were yesterday."

Thank you, thank you, God.

I said to Dave, "Oh, fanks, Dave. You are indeedy a pal of the first water."

"And sexy beyond words."

"And... sexy beyond words."

Phoned Jas.

"Jas, he didn't get in touch with Thongy, he just sent a postcard to Dom, and Wet Lindsay pretended that he had got in touch with her! Hahahahaha. How pathetico she is. *Hasta la vista*, baby!!"

I slammed down the phone so that Jas couldn't spoil my mood by rambling on about Hunky.

Oh, I luuurve life!

And the Italian Stallion.

And I quite like Dave the Laugh.

In a laughy way.

If I have time in between snogging, I may send him a postcard.

11:20 a.m.

He actually asked for an American cheerleader or a ranch, but he was just being silly.

12:10 p.m.

Ditherspaz attack on the clothes front.

♥ 91

I said to Mum as she came in to hand me some clean "panties", "I have not got one single thing to wear."

She didn't even bother to reply, she just looked meaningfully at my two cases, one of which I was sitting on to try and make it shut.

12:20 p.m.
Maybe one set of boy entrancers will be enough to last me the week? That would save a bit of space.

12:24 p.m.
Nope, I still can't shut the lid of one of my suitcases.

Vati has relented and let me take two cases, but he will have a nervy b if I ask for another one.

Maybe I can make do with just eight pairs of shoes.

Oh, the tension, the tension.

12:30 p.m.
There was a horrible scratching and banging against my bedroom door. Angus was doing his paws-under-the-door thing. Oh God.

I said, "Go away, Angus, this is a cat-free zone."

I'm not having him in here dropping his bat ears and so on on my clean things.

12:45 p.m.
He will not go away. If I didn't know better, I would say that he sensed we're going away. This is driving me insane. Now Gordy is putting his paws under the door as well.

I got up and opened the door. Gordy was on his back wriggling around with his pretend mouse pal, but Angus was just sitting there looking at me with his tongue lolling out. And foam coming out of his mouth.

Honestly.

The foam was frothing all over his face and dripping on to the carpet.

My God, he's got rabies!

1:00 p.m.
It turns out that Angus has eaten his bath-time soap.

2:00 p.m.
Hurrah hurrah and total result! Grandvati has given me twenty squids for my holidays.

Vati said, "Oh well, that is a score less than I have to give you."

Is he mad?

I said to Mutti, "Mum, that's not fair, is it? I mean... it means that Grandvati hasn't really given me twenty squids. No, what it means is this: Grandvati HAS given me twenty squids out of his little tiny tiny pension-type money and Dad has STOLEN it from him. And another thing..."

2:15 p.m.

Relentless moaning strikes again!

Vati yelled at me, "Go on, then. Go and waste the money, just don't give a second thought to the hours it takes me to make the damn stuff."

I said, "Okey-dokey, I won't."

As I went out of the door to go and spendies my squids, I said, "S'later, Mum. I don't know whether to get another mood ring or a piercing."

I slammed the door before my father could explode.

6:30 p.m.

Two new lippies and a flavoured lip gloss. I wonder if Masimo likes strawberry flavour. I've got raspberry as well.

Maybe I should mix them for that fruit-cocktail-type snogging experience. Perhaps I should have got some custard flavour lip gloss, too. Shutup brain.

7:00 p.m.
Loon village round at my house.

Jas has come round to stay overnight. Her eyes are like little piggie eyes because of the bye-bye Hunky scenario. What a great laugh (NOT) she is going to be. I'm sure she'll perk up, though, when we're driving through Hamburger-a-gogo and she gets the smell of bucking broncos and beans in her nostrils.

Jas's dad actually SAID something when he dropped her off! He said, "Take care, my little love. Have a great time."

And then he said this really really touching thing to Jas that nearly made me weep. He said, "Here's a bit of extra cash; get something nice."

7:10 p.m.
It was Hug City when Mr and Mrs Jas left. Unfortunately it started Jas on an uncontrollable crying jag AGAIN. She is going to have to be more rufty tufty if she wants to survive this Vale of Tears we call life.

7:30 p.m.

Mutti has made us an unusually normal and nutritious meal, and Jas managed to stop sniffling enough to stuff down forty-five pounds of shepherd's pie.

My bedroom
8:30 p.m.

We are doing our last-minute emergency packing check. It's not made very easy by Gordy pouncing on my hand every time I move it. I will be damn glad when Gordy can run free and wild. He will be allowed out when we get back, and he can get rid of his pent-up kittykat aggression on the Prat Poodles and voles and so on.

As I predicted, Jas has got an insane amount of "panties" with her. I said, "Are you expecting a worldwide famine on the botty-hugger front?"

But she was rambling on about Hunky again. "What if he meets someone else in Kiwi-a-gogo land? A Maori or something?"

Before I could join in she went raving on. "He's given me a love token. Do you want to see it?"

"Jas, if it's some sort of secret tattoo thing like last time, I don't really want to see—"

I might just as well have been speaking to myself.

"It's a sort of secret tattoo thing. Like last time. Look."

Is it normal to have a secret tattoo of two voles kissing? No, is the answer you are looking for. Jas has one though.

On her bottom.

Suddenly the enormous botty huggers make all kinds of sense to me.

"Tom made the tracing in technical drawing and then he inked it in. He's got a similar one on his—"

"Jas, Jas... please leave it out. I am trying to make sure I haven't forgotten anything essential – like something to kill you with."

But secretly I am vair vair happy because I am almost on the LUUURVE Trail and nothing Jas does can upset me.

I said, "Stop thinking about Hunky now. We must have a plan. As soon as we land we'll get a bus timetable to see what bus we must catch for Manhattan."

"You have to catch a Greyhound."

"Jas, I am not riding a dog all the way to New York."

"It's an American bus-type thingy, and anyway, I am not going to Manhattan."

"Yes you are, Jazzy Spazzy."

"No I'm not."

"Yes you are."

"No I'm not."

"Jas, if you go on being so vair vair silly, I will have to confiscate some of your botty huggers."

She got the megahump then and wouldn't even cheer up when I made an amusing hat out of her pink-spotted panties.

8:45 p.m.

There was a mad ringing at the door.

It was Grandvati and his "girlfriend" Maisie. I said hello to the elderly loons, and when they went off into the front room to talk to Dad about their cat duties, I followed Mum into her bedroom.

She said, "I'm really looking forward to this trip, aren't you? I wonder if we will bump into George Clooney. I hope we do! He's so... woof woof."

I said, "Mum, excuse me if I'm right, but did you just bark like a dog?"

She laughed. "Well, you know, he's gorgeous isn't he?

And he might really like English women."

"Mum, do you really think it's likely that George Clooney is going to be at a clown-car convention?"

Mum said, "Well, he's got lots of hobbies; he's got a pet pig."

I despair for her sanity.

To bring her back down to real life I asked her something that had been bothering me a lot. "I hope that you'll tell Grandad that Maisie can't stay overnight. We don't want our reputation tarnished."

Mum laughed, but not in an amused way.

I said, "Well, at least hide the matches."

She ignored me as she zipped up her suitcase, singing the theme to *ER*. She clearly is dreaming about driving around with George in a clown car. Possibly with his pet pig as chauffeur. Like a porky Parker.

9:00 p.m.
Next to arrive was Uncle Eddie. Joy unbounded. Uncle Eddie has a Hawaiian shirt like Dad's. Hurrah! I'm going on holiday with two porky surfers.

Uncle Eddie gave Dad a high five and said, "Hello hello hello, big up for the lads."

Oh Lordy Lordy.

I went to the loo, and when I came back into the room, Dad, Uncle Eddie and Grandad were wearing blond Afro wigs.

Why?

It all became hideously clear when Dad said, "Let the 'Hello America' Abba tribute begin!"

Oh nooo.

9:15 p.m.

Jas and me are holed up in my room while the grown-ups are singing "Waterloo". I said to her, "This is a good opportunity for you to nip downstairs and start ringing people in New York, New York called Scarlotti."

She didn't even bother to stop straightening her fringe.

9:28 p.m.

Another ring of the doorbell.

Sound out the bells of England, it was the Ace Gang. Yesssss!!! Even Jas forgot she was having a grumpathon.

Jools, Rosie, Mabs and Ellen all gave the time-honoured Klingon salute.

Rosie said, "We're not staying because we're going to the Catfish for a bop, but we have come with a message of wisdomosity."

Oooohhh, how sweet.

They said all together, "Have a good time ALL of the time."

And then Rosie said, "*Bon voyage* and also Bon Jovi. See you in the next life; don't be late."

One farewell burst of disco inferno dancing and they were gone.

In the hall
9:30 p.m.

Jas went back to her fringe-straightening duties in my bedroom, but as the olds were singing along to "Dancing Queen" I quickly phoned international directory enquiries. The lady operator had clearly not been facilitated into the mystery of helpfulnosity, because when I politely said, "Good evening, would you connect me to anyone in New York, New York who has the surname Scarlotti?" she said, "Don't be so bloody silly." and put the phone down.

This is what the British Empire has come to.

In bed
11:05 p.m.

Jas needn't have gone to all the trouble of making a lesbian barrier of pillows, because Libby has got into bed between us. She is looking from one to the other of us, smiling, with no front teeth.

I don't trust this smiling business.

Libby was turning her head from side to side looking at Jas and then looking at me. I must make her go to sleep.

I said, "Night-night then, Bibsy, time for Boboland. Shall I sing you a little night-time song?"

"No."

Ten minutes later

She won't stop turning her head from side to side, saying, "Naaaiiice, naaiiice." It's very unnerving.

Thirty seconds later

She's just suddenly fallen asleep. Just kajonk. Asleep. No yawning, just unconscious. How strange is that? How do they do that, the toddly-type people – the instant-falling-asleep thing?

Jas whispered to me, "I will never get to sleep. I'm just thinking and thinking about Tom."

Twenty seconds later

And now she's just fallen asleep! She is vair vair superficial.

Oh God. Anyway, I am never going to get to sleep either as I'm so excited beyond the Valley of the Excited and into the Universe... zzzzzzzzzzzzzzzzzz.

Howdy, Hamburger-a-gogo land! Brace yourselves for a knicker invasion!!!

Sunday May 22nd
8:30 a.m.

Cor, we are quite literally up at the crack of dawn.

I had no sooner slumped into a dream about my lips turning into hamburgers and Masimo spreading some tomato sauce on them than Mum was shaking me awake.

She was dressed in some new jeans, which I have never seen before and never want to see again.

"Mum, do they like the prostitute look in Hamburger-a-gogo?"

Mum said, "Don't start."

But I am not wrong.

9:00 a.m.

Up and dressed in my travelling outfit. Finally decided on my pale-blue ribbed T-shirt, cool jeans and pearl-buckle leather belt, with my highest-heeled shoes. (The highest heels allowed by the fascist fashion *kommandant*, aka, my dad.) I have some ballet slippers to put on later so that I don't get deep vein whatsit, as Vati is too mean to spend an extra thousand pounds so that I can have a chair that turns into a little bed on the plane. As I said to Mum, "A thousand pounds is just TOO much to spend to ensure his daughter will walk again, but there you are."

I left Jas trying to decide which botty huggers to wear for comfortabilitynessnosity on the plane, and went to say goodbye to the kittykats.

We have managed to convince Libby that they are not flying with us because they are coming on the special cat plane, which has little cat baskets instead of seats. And, I must say, it was my bit about them having their own little video sets by their baskets showing films of dogs being chased by cats that did the trick. It amused Libby so much, I thought she was going to have a fit.

9:15 a.m.

Gordon should be under strict house arrest, but he has done a dash for freedom and is on the wall with his father. I notice that the anti-cat fence has been partially eaten.

Angus playfully biffed me around the head when I went over to them. Gordy rolled over on to his back and looked at me upside down. I tickled his little tummy – sooooo cute. Then he locked all his paws round my hand and stuck his claws into me. Owwwww! I tried to get him off, but he is very strong for a little kittykat. He wouldn't even let go when I lifted him off the wall and he just hung there on the end of my hand. I shook him off at last, and he spun round in the air and landed on all of his little paws. Excellent tail work on the landing.

Angus was looking sleepily down at his offspring, probably thinking, *I have taught that boy everything he knows.*

As I got eye-level with the big furry loony, he looked straight at me. He has the most yellow mad eyes you have ever seen, but in his own way I think he loves me. That is what I think. It was like he was looking deep down into my soul, thinking, *Yes, we are different creatures, but we*

have a bond deep down inside. You are a baldy fool who cannot even catch her own snacks, but we both have hearts and appendixes. And neither of us have trouser-snake addendas."

A touching telepathic speech from him because usually he is not very talkative.

I said, "Bye-bye, Angus. I love you and I will be back."

He put his paw out and just patted at my nose really gently.

I think he understands every word I say and this is his way of saying "s'later".

9:25 a.m.

As we drove out of our driveway in Dad's friend's white van, Grandad yelled out to us, "Have a lovely time, and Georgia, try and get on with people!"

That's nice, isn't it?

I said to everyone, "That's a bit rich coming from a convicted convict, isn't it?" But no one heard me above the singing.

Even Libby was joining in with "Get off of my blue suede shoes". Or in her case, "Get offer my blue snail shoes".

9:30 a.m.

On our way to the airport of luuurve dreams. I am sooooo excited. I said to Jas, "I am going to call all the people who have the same surname as Masimo as soon as we get to whatsitsname."

Jas said, "Memphis."

"Yes, that."

In the departure lounge

11:00 a.m.

I said to Jas, "Hamburger-a-gogo land, here we come! Brace yourselves for a knicker invasion!!!"

12:00 p.m.

Mutti was sooo nervy about taking off. She is still holding my hand and she has only just let go of the bloke across the aisle's hand. He looks a bit apprehensive, and not entirely sane. Mutti, me, Jas, Libby, scuba-diving Barbie and Sandra are all sitting next to each other, and Uncle Eddie and Vati have seats in front of us. The man across the aisle offered to change seats with Dad so he could sit across from Mum but Dad said, "You wouldn't be safe next to my friend. We call him The Prince of Darkness at home. He needs very careful managing." Then Uncle Eddie looked back at the man, with two plastic spoons stuck up his nose. Why?

The Prince of Darkness and his porky pal, my vati, have already embarrassed themselves by ordering ridiculous cocktails with umbrellas in them. And flirting with the air hostesses. It is vair vair sad. If they start singing and putting on their Elvis quiffs, I will go mad. I suppose Dad imagines his leather trousers make him look like a groover. I said to Mum, "Was Vati meaning to look like a transvestite?" But she was fiddling about with her seat-belt.

She said, "Do you think I could get an extra one? This doesn't look very sturdy, does it?"

"I wouldn't bother about your belt, Mum, this aeroplane must weigh about a million tons, and that little belt is not going to save you when we nose-dive two miles into the Atlantic."

She said, "Shut up," which I don't think is very caring. However, live and let live. And also let the spirit of holidaynosity and Luuurvegoddosity run rife through the aisles of life, is what I say.

Jas, who is wearing her "travelling outfit", i.e., some

enormous joggers and pigtails, said, "Do you remember the captain on the boat when we went on the school trip to Froggyland?"

"Jas, how could I ever forget Captain Mad? We were lucky to crash into France, otherwise we would be still there going round and—"

Then the plane's captain came on the tannoy.

"Gud evening, ladies and gents, we're awae on our trip to Memphis, and hoots a clear nacht the noo."

Dear God. He was from Och Aye land.

I clutched Mum and said, "We're all doomed. Doomed, I tell you."

Which I thought was quite funny. Mum didn't.

Two hours later

Rollers in for bouceability hairwise. We checked first that there were no fit boys on the flight. Not, as I said to Jas, that I am remotely interested. I said, "I am eschewing the General Horn and red-bottomosity with a firm hand, but you never know."

Dad turned round when he smelled the nail polish (I decided to change Pouting Pink for Go Baby) and saw us in our rollers. After he had stopped laughing, he and Uncle Eddie amused themselves by pretending we were space creatures. Dad kept showing us things and saying, "Spoon, do not be afraid. This is a SPOON." Then they'd go back to talking rubbish, and a few minutes later Dad would turn round with a fork to show us.

Vair vair amusing.

How we laughed.

Not.

Libby is in Libbyland making scuba-diving Barbie and Sandra do "snoggling". If Sandra wasn't in fact our Lord in a dress, it would be lezzie snogging. I blame my parents because of their lack of moral code.

Mum has relaxed enough to start her usual flirting with anything in trousers. She almost wet herself when the bloke across the aisle (Randy) asked her if she had been a child bride. (I told you he was mad.)

When she nipped off to apply yet more make-up, I leaned over her seat to talk to Randy. "Er, howdy. Do you know anyone called Masimo Scarlotti in Manhattan?"

Randy looked as if he was a rabbit caught in a car's headlights. He was vair vair nervous for no reason.

♥ III

Eventually he said, "Well, er, Manhattan is a big place and..."

I smiled. "I don't think an eighth of an inch mapwise is that big really."

He just looked at me.

I said to Jas quietly, "I don't think that Randy has all the buttons on his cardigan, if you know what I mean."

But I gave him the benefit of the doubtosity. I smiled at him and he took a big glug of his vodka.

An hour later

Still on this sodding plane somewhere in the Atlantic.

The captain keeps telling us to put our watches back an hour; it's more like having a clock driving than a person.

Fifteen thousand hours, or something

Or is that our height?

I said to Jas, "Have we crossed the International Date Line yet? Are we going backwards or forwards through time? It could be 1066 for all we know."

Jas is reading her ludicrous fungi book so she didn't even bother to answer.

Half an hour later

Or perhaps half an hour sooner. Who knows?

The captain came and walked down the aisle saying hello to people. He was not what I would call a confidence-inducing sight, although at least he wasn't wearing a kilt. He looked close to eighty-five. Also, he bumped into an air hostess, so maybe he has failing eyesight. Or at the least, very bad spatial awareness.

As the captain passed by us, Mum said, "Is everything all right, Captain?"

And he winked. Honestly. A million miles up in the air with no visible means of support and you have a winker in charge. He said, "Aye, madam, it's gud weather for flying."

Libby looked at him and smiled her tongue-through-the-teeth smile.

"Heggo mister man, give me and my fwends naaaiice sweeties."

Mum said, "Libby, naughty girl, the captain is too busy to—"

But the captain had clearly never had any experience of the bonkers toddly folk because he said, "Come on, then, little lassie, let's see what we can find for ye."

Two minutes later

Libby lobes the captain. She is sitting on his knee at the back of the plane, singing him her poo song. He's joining in.

Mum was looking back and smiling and saying to me, "Aaaahh, that's sweet, isn't it?"

There was a bit of a pause and then she yelled, "Oh my God, who is driving the plane?!!!"

Touchdown

Miraculously we have landed safely. After making such a fuss about everything, Mum fell asleep. In fact all of the grown-ups were unconscious when we landed in Memphis.

Jas was checking her watch as we took our rollers out. She said, "Isn't it weird that it's more or less the same time as when we took off, and that we landed yesterday as far as Hunky is concerned?"

Good grief, I needn't have bothered about day to evening wear.

However, I have got maximus voluminosity and bounceability on the hair front.

I may write a book on international beauty tips.

Memphis airport

Howdy, Hamburger-a-gogo land! Let the Luuurve Trail commence!!!

Jas and I did a tribute disco inferno dance when we got off the plane.

Twenty minutes later

Waiting for our luggage.

I haven't seen anyone who hasn't got a moustache yet.

And, frankly, that is not attractive in a woman.

Customs

I was singing "Head 'em up, round 'em up, head 'em out, rawhide. Head 'em up, round 'em up head 'em out, rawhide rawhiiiiiiiiiide" in an amusing and entertaining way as we got our stuff and trundled along to customs, but it was, I have to say, not going down very well. In fact it was like being in Hawkeye City.

The customs man asked me if I was bringing in any livestock. I thought he was having a laugh, so I said, "Only, as you see, my father and his mate."

He wasn't having a laugh.

Not at all.

In our rental car

A willing-but-dim Hamburger-a-gogo chap (with a moustache) showed us to a massive black limo-type scenario. It was called a "Mustang" or "Arsekicker" or something. Anyway, it was big as a big thing. Dad and Uncle Eddie were ecstatic, kicking the tyres and so on – it is vair vair sad. The W-but-D chap said, "This is your vee-hick-el, sir. Now, you all drive safely, you hear?"

What was he going on about?

What is a vee-hick-el?

Jas said, "Does he mean a vehicle?"

I said, "Get loose, Jazzy Spazzy. Who cares as long as the vee-hick-el is a Luuurve vee-hick-el. Prepare to enter the vee-hick-el. Adjust your knickers; we are on our way!!"

After a million years of Dad fiddling with keys, we got into one of the eighty-five million seats inside and snuggled down while Vati and Uncle Eddie twiddled with their knobs.

I hugged Jazzy. And amazingly she hugged me back.

I said, "Jas, I am sooo excited, aren't you?"

She said, "Ooh look, there's a little TV on the back of the seat!"

As the Thunderbird-a-gogo or whatever it was took off at one mile an hour, driven by Dad, I said to Jas, "I can almost smell Masimo."

She said, "Oo-er."

And then we both fell about laughing. I think I have got hysterical jet lag.

Dad and Uncle Eddie were singing "I left my heart in San Franciso" and have already started yelling "howdy" out of the window at anyone we pass.

It's only a matter of time before they are taken to jail. So things are looking up.

4:00 p.m. timewise

I think someone forgot to mention something to me. It's HUGE here! The buildings, the signs, the shorts. Everything is HUGE here. And bloody hot. I'd ask Dad to turn on the air conditioning if I didn't know what a waste of time that would be; he's already opened the sun roof ten times when he was trying to change gears. And more to the point, there ISN'T a gear stick; this is an automatic car.

4:30 p.m.

Fifty million years of swaying about in the back of a vee-hick-el driven by someone who doesn't know what side of the road is the right one (and that's when we are in England). It was only when we passed the same group of people for the fifth time and they started waving and cheering that Dad let Uncle Eddie drive.

Hotel

5:00 p.m.

This is more like it. A huge driveway lined with hibiscus and palm trees and a fountain and then a hotel with about fifty-six floors. Tip-top hotel life. As soon as we screeched to a halt a millimetre away from the fountain, some chap in a uniform opened the car doors. He seemed vair vair cheerful, like someone had told him a really good joke. Perhaps he had heard about the clown-car convention, or seen Uncle Eddie trying to park. He smiled and clapped his hands and said, "Well, how are you all doing? Come on in, come on in! Welcome to Memphis, folks. The home of Elvis. But this is not Heartbreak Hotel, no siree – this is YOUR hotel!"

Good Lord. I said to Uncle Eddie really quietly, "Put your

foot down and drive like the wind."

But Mr Smiley Mad Pants had already taken all our bags inside. Still grinning like he was really pleased to see us.

The receptionist (Candi) practically split her mouth in half, she was smiling and saying "alrighty" so much.

While Dad and Uncle Eddie sorted out the rooms, Mum said, "Aren't they all just, you know..."

I said, "Bonkers?"

Mum got all mumish. "No, aren't they all so nice? Let's have a little look at the pool."

Poolsidewise

Wowzee wow and also yee-hah!! Fabby pool all surrounded by palm trees and with miniature waterfalls and stuff. We tried out the sun lounger things. Libby gave Sandy and scuba-diving Barbie a bit of privacy by putting them on their own special lounger.

As soon as we sat down a waitress dashed over. Blimey. Sometimes *days* can go by in English restaurants before some complete fool comes ambling over to take your order, and then tells you they haven't got it.

Our waitress (Loreen) was beside herself with joy at

seeing us and said, "Well, howdy to you all, thank you for coming to Memphis. Can I get you ladies anything?"

Mum said, "Could I have tea for four, and perhaps a couple of ham sandwiches if that's not too much trouble?"

Loreen slapped her thigh, laughed for about a year and said, "With that cute accent you can have anything you want, ma'am."

Mum said to Libby, "Bibs, would you like a little ham sandwich?"

Libby looked at the waitress and started snorting and grunting and pretending to be a mad piglet. "Hoggy hoggy, piggy sandwich!"

And Loreen chuckled and said, "Now aren't you the cutest?"

Cutest?

Libby?

Good Lord.

Ten minutes later

Jas is writing a postcard to Hunky. We've only been here a minute. She has no pridenosity.

Mum started taking her jacket off. I said, "I beg you,

Mum, do not alarm anyone with your nungas."

She is in such a good mood, and obviously expecting to see George Clooney any minute, that she just smiled at me and lay back in her chair.

Jas said, "I wonder what time it is in Kiwi-a-gogo. If we are six hours back from England and New Zealand is twelve hours ahead of England, that means... erm... let me see."

I said, "Jas please work it out in your head and don't start talking about minutes to me. It makes my brain go jelloid."

Once I have had a snack, I will have the strength to get on the phone to the Luuurve God.

Fifteen minutes later

Loreen has arrived with our "snack". My sandwich is made out of two loaves of bread, chips, a huge gherkin and a piglet.

Loreen said to Libby, who was gnawing her way through forty pounds of ham, "Is that alrighty for you, Miss Beautiful?"

Pardon?

Then, attracted by the gnawing, Cindi, a waitress with eight-foot hair came over and said, "Now you leave her

♡ 121

alone, Loreen; she is mine." Then they had a bit of a mock mini fight over Libby, shouting, "Now you give her here, she is miiiiine."

Quite quite weird.

We sat there chewing as Loreen and Cindi sort of pushed each other around. Finally Loreen won and she picked up Libby and gave her a cuddle.

Libby didn't hit her.

I was amazed.

We were all amazed.

It was amazing, that's why.

She was cuddling my sister; my sister wasn't biffing her.

Now Loreen was kissing Sandra. Blimey.

Then some bloke passing by with twenty-five pounds of sausages on his plate stopped and joined in. "How are y'all folks doing?"

I said, "We're doing as alrighty as... er... alrighty things, thank you."

And he said, "Hey, miss, are you from Ireland? Well, begorrah you are real pretty and you have a sparkling personality. Now you all take care and have a nice day."

Mum practically choked on her pig's leg.

Half an hour of alrighty time later

After our "snack" we staggered to the elevator and a complete stranger in tartan slacks and matching hat said, as he got out, "Now you enjoy Memphis, you hear?"

On the way up to our room I said to Jas, "What do they want from us?"

Inside

Mum went off with Libby into the "family" room and Jas and me went into our room. I heard Libby saying to Mum, "When is the kittykat plane landing, Mummmmmeeeeee?"

Oh dear.

Our room

Wow and wowzee wow! It was HUGE! And it had its own private bathroom. No more chance sightings of my parents in the nuddy-pants.

When we got to our room the bellhop was putting our bags on one of the ginormous beds.

I said, "Oh, thank you very much."

And he slapped his thigh and said, "Now where are you all from?"

I said, "Erm, we're all from England."

And he did a bit of a dance and said, "Say something in British."

I looked at Jas, but she was busy walking in and out of the walk-in wardrobe.

It was really making me nervy having an ogling person ogling me from about an inch away from my head. Especially one who thinks that I speak British. Anyway, I said, "Do you know if there's a bus that goes to Manhattan, please?"

And he started hooting with laugher. I was just looking at him. Eventually he managed to wipe his eyes and calm down and went cackling off out of the room.

Jas said, "Georgie, look, there's like a cupboard thing with drinks and snacks in."

I said, "Oh thank God!"

But I was being ironic because I am so full of piglet I can barely move.

We lay on our ginormous beds and made a plan.

I said, "OK, the first thing is... we phone up directory enquiries and... zzzzzzzzzzzzzzzzzz."

Monday May 23rd
8:30 a.m.

What in the name of arse happened? I remember putting on the TV and Mum and Dad coming in and saying, "We are just going to have a little zizz." I thought, *Hahahaha, now is my chance. I will just lie on my ginormous bed and have a little rest to perk me up for my phone call to the Luuurve God.* And then it was now. If you see what I mean.

But hey hey hey, this is our official first morning in Hamburger-a-gogo land!

Jas was awake, looking at me, in her giant sleeping knicker ensemble and giant bed.

I said, "Howdy," and she said, "Alrighty," and I said, "Goddamn rootin' tootin' I'm alrighty."

And we laughed like loons in Loonland, which we are.

9:00 a.m. Hamburgertimewise

Jas was looking out of our two-hundred-millionth floor window, and I said, "Any sign of cowboys?"

She said, "No, but I can see some bloke doing nuddy-pants gardening on a roof."

Wowzee wow!! I leaped out of bed and went to the

♡ 125

window, and there was Mr Rudey Dudey Nudey on the roof of another hotel!

I said, "Boo, he's wearing tiny swimming knickers, or swimming 'panties', as we must say to get along with people here. I'm going to use our phone to call up Masimo in Manhattan."

Jas said, "Good luck. Hey, I wonder if I could phone Tom in Kiwi-a-gogo."

It was really groovy having our own phone for once.

I said to Jas, "What is the codey-type thing for Manhattan?"

Typically, Jas didn't know. I don't know what the point of coming top in history is if you don't even know the simplest thing, but I didn't say that because I am vair nearly in Luuurve Heaven City.

I phoned reception and an alarmingly cheerful person said, "Gayleen speaking, how can I help you, ma'am?"

"Oh... er... I would like to make a call to Manhattan please."

"You got it. Now you just wait, ma'am while I connect you to the appropriate party."

This was more like it. I said to Jas, "This is why I luuurve the American-type people. They DO stuff for you. Also, they are very truthful – you know, like last night that bloke said I was beautiful and had a sparkling personality. That is why I like them, because they are full of sinceriosity!"

...And that is when Dad answered the phone.

"Dad!"

"Oh, yes. I wondered how long it would be before you were on the phone to your mates, telling them what you're having for breakfast and what colour lipstick you might wear."

Donner and Blitzen!

And *merde*!!

And also DARN!!!

Even on holiday, Dad is so mad and unreasonable. He has told the hotel to put all our calls through to him!

I said to him, "What if I needed to call the emergency services?"

"I could call them."

"But what if you had, er... fallen over your shorts and—"

"Georgia, shut up and just accept that you are not calling your mates on the hotel phone. You can use your own money in a phone box." Then he hung up.

♡

Sacré bleu.

The phone rang. It was Vati again.

"And don't even think about eating anything out of the room bar or using room service without my permission."

What was this? A holiday or Stalag 14 on tour?

Through the Fat Controller (Dad), Jas and I ordered the "healthy option" breakfast.

Fifteen minutes later

Jas and me were sitting in the bath watching the mini TV on the shelf by the sink. It's like on a stem thing and you can twist it around so you can watch it from any angle, even on the loo. (By the way, we were sitting in the bath not in a lezzie way, just in a in-our-jimjams-way.)

There was a knock at the door, and our "healthy option" breakfasts arrived.

I don't know whose idea of a healthy option it was, but in my book twenty-five tons of porridge, four eggs and forty pounds of fried potatoes plus toast doesn't suggest health to me – it suggests death.

The smiling person (Dolly) who brought us the brekkie tray said, "Now you all have a nice day, you hear?"

128

And I didn't even say, "No, YOU all have a nice day."

I have never been smiled at by a waitress in my life until I got here.

Creepy.

I said to Jas, "What is it these people want?"

11:30 a.m.

We all climbed into the Loonmobile to go and explore Memphis. Uncle Eddie and Vati were wearing baseball hats backwards with their false Elvis quiffs sticking out of the front. There was no need for it. I said to Dad, "Dad, we are representing Her Maj the Queen, and quite frankly you two are doing a really crap job."

Uncle Eddie, once again at the "controls", accelerated away so suddenly that we were forced back in our seats – like that G-force thing. Only in our case it was the Uncle Baldy force.

As we careered along, there were signs all over saying, "Elvis the King dared to rock!" and so on. Every time they saw one, Dad and Uncle Eddie would start singing another Elvis song and moving their shoulders about and saying "Uh-huh".

I must find a phone box and set off to Manhattan as soon as I can.

Out of the Loonmobile and amazingly still alive

Memphis is blindingly hot and sort of groovy in a really loony groovy way. Everywhere you go there are Elvis songs blasting out of cafés and bars and shops, and people dressed up as him. I never thought the day would come when I would say this, but Dad and Uncle Eddie were almost sane-looking in comparison to some. Is it normal for old ladies who are fifty-eight stone to dress in rhinestone jumpsuits and false black sidies? "No", I think, is the answer you are searching for.

The grown-ups were all keen on going to look at Robinmobile Headquarters on the outskirts of town. I said to mum, "Please, please don't make me and Jas go. Please, we're only young, we have our whole lives ahead of us. Please, please."

Eventually they agreed that we could have a look round town and they would go "check the scene", as Dad pathetically put it, wiggling his dark glasses. Dear God.

As they went off he said, "Be back here, outside Elvis's

Rock Emporium, in two hours or say goodbye to ever going out by yourselves again."

Cheers.

But at least we were free!!!

As they went off and got back into the car, we waved and looked full of maturiosity. Then, when Uncle Eddie had careered round the corner in the Thunderbird thing, we did thumbsie upsies and a swift disco inferno.

I yelled, "Yes and three times yes!!! Goodbye, porky ones! We are off on the Luuurve Train! Or Luuurve Greyhound!!!"

Jas said, "I am not getting on a bus to Manhattan with you. And that is final."

I put my arm around her. "Come on, my bestest little pally, one for all and all for one and all for me."

"No."

"Jas—"

"No."

I resisted the temptation to kick her stupid legs, and decided to use my famous charmosity. "Jas, let us just go and find a phone box. I can phone Masimo and say, "Ciao Masimo, your dreamboat has landed." and you can phone Hunky and ask him how many boring... er, I mean how many fascinating bits of wombat poo he has found in Kiwi-a-gogo and so on."

Jas perked up then. "Oh yeah, I could... unless you think it's sort of... well, you know, keen... but I am keen, aren't I? And I have got his phone number – well, at least I've got the number of the farm he's staying on."

Good Lord. She is soooo, you know, pathetico.

And I say that with deep loveosity.

We had to wait to cross the road with the other Memphis-type people. One enormously friendly person, who clearly had "eaten all the pies", said there was a phone box in the "drugstore". Can you imagine it being called that in Shakespeare-a-gogo land? Anyway, as we waited at the lights they changed, and instead of the "Beep beep beep" thing, it had a woman talking in a Memphis accent. Honestly! She said, "Now you all are safe to cross the road."

A shop next to the drugstore had a notice on its door that said, "No drinking, eating or firearms in the shop."

Wow!

In the drugstore

We asked the drugstore man how to use his telephone thing. He gave us loads of quarters or something. I couldn't quite make out what he was saying, as he was eating a hamburger at the time. I did hear him say, "Are you going to phone Her Majesty at BuckingHAM Palace?"

What was he talking about?

Telephone box

The telephone was a bit low. Are there a lot of tiny people in Memphis? I was a bit phased about asking the operator for numbers in Manhattan on my first go at the phoney thing, so I thought I would try phoning Rosie.

Jas was looning about being an unhelp. I said, "Are they five hours ahead?"

And she said, "Well, if it's yesterday tomorrow in Kiwi-a-gogo, well, that makes it... er..."

As she was rambling on I picked up the receiver and it made a really funny dialling noise, and then I had to shove in tons of quarters. Then it made a funny ringing-type noise. It was almost like I was in a foreign country.

Perhaps no one was in.

Then Rosie answered the phone.

Yesssssss and three times yesssss!!! Contact!

England! England! A person who spoke my own language at last!

Rosie said, "Bonsoir."

"Ro Ro, it's me and Jas!"

Jas was trying to get the receiver off me and yelling, "Let me say hello. Let me."

Vair annoying.

I let her have a go, though, because I wanted her to do stuff for me. She was ludicrously excited, like we had been away for years in the Antarctic and had just found a phone on an ice floe.

"Rosie, it's me, Jas, in Hamburger-a-gogo!"

She rambled on for ages, saying stuff like, "What is the weather like there? Oh, is it? Raining? Is it that light rain that soaks you right through? Yeah? Right. Not really raining, more like spitting? It still wets you right through, though, doesn't it? It's boiling here. The money is different." Really really boring stuff. For ages.

I said, "Give me a go, Jas, before the money runs out."

She handed the phone over to me. I said, "Ro Ro, guess

how many people over here have said they love me?"

And Rosie said, "None?"

Happy days. Back to normality.

I luuurve my friends. Rosie is growing dreadlocks and Sven has had his thumb pierced.

After we had said goodbye to Rosie, Jas went off into another booth to speak to Hunky.

I took a deep breath got my coins ready and got through to the operator.

Fifteen minutes later

Do you know how many Scarlottis there are in Manhattan?

A million.

I could spend the rest of my life phoning them.

Jas came out of her tiny-person's booth to get more change, and I said, "It's bloody hopeless. There are about a billion people called Scarlotti in Manhattan."

She said, "Why don't you use sort of psychic luuurve bonding and just telepathically think of where he will be and choose that number?"

Fifteen minutes later

I have made many many new Hamburgese friends, all called Scarlotti. One of them seemed a bit on the Chinese side and I think I may have ordered egg fried rice to go, but that is life. Oh, I have laughed, I have cried with my new mates, I have talked about central heating and so on, but I have not spoken to anyone who knows Masimo. And I have spent almost all my money.

Jas was still on the phone, nodding like a nodding thing.

Huh, she was probably doing pretend snogging on the phone to Hunky.

I was exhausted.

I went up to the counter and ordered myself a milkshake.

The young chap wanted to talk. Oh dear. He said, "Now, where are you all from?"

I said, "England."

He said, "Oh wow... awesome."

He was just looking at me drinking my milkshake.

Then he said, "Do you know Prince Charles?"

Oh dear God.

I said, "Yes, I play table tennis with him."

Fortunately, or unfortunately, depending how you look at

it, Jas came and sat down beside me.

I said, "I have spoken to loads of people, pretty much all of them mad, and spent all my money and I have no idea where Masimo is. What about you? How was Hunky?"

"I don't know. I've just been told off for about a million years."

It turns out that when Jas eventually got through to the farm it was 1:00 a.m timewise and the Kiwi-a-gogo farmer who eventually answered wasn't pleased.

Jas said, "When he answered the phone he said, 'Are you there?' You know, with that funny accent that goes up at the end."

"Why did he say 'Are you there?' when you had just phoned him?"

"I don't know, it's the Kiwi-a-gogo way."

"Then what happened?"

"I said, 'Yes, I am here, are you there?' and he lost his rag for no reason and said, 'Don't go playing the bloody smartarse with me.' and started giving me a lecture about how hard they worked on the farm and what time they all had to be up. I said, 'Er, I'm in Memphis,' and he said, 'I don't care if you're in the bloody body of a whale, don't phone up in the middle of the bloody night.'" And he put the phone down on her.

Crikey.

I never intended to go to Kiwi-a-gogo, and now I know I made the right decision. Do you know why? Because they are all mad.

And they think that just gone midnight is late.

I rest my case.

Jas was all miffed, but she agreed to just have a look at the bus station. We shuffled off to find it. Hot as billio. I think I am getting a bit brown though. Everyone is soooo friendly, it's vair vair tiring. And all the men wear either Elvis costumes or dungarees.

I said to Jas to cheer her up, "I have never seen grown men wear dungarees."

She said, "They're not called dungarees in Hamburger-a-gogo land, they're called overalls."

I looked at her.

"How come you know so much about it? Have you got some?"

She went a bit Jasish. "Well, yes, I, er... use them for, you know, er... gardening and so on. They have many useful pockets."

Yes, I bet.

I had a sudden image of her and Tom cavorting around in her bedroom in their dungarees...

Bus station

Do you know when buses go to Manhattan? Never, that's when. Also, if they did go, it would take five weeks to get there and back.

Sacré bleu.

Jas said, "Look, be reasonable. We are not going to track him down, let's just try and enjoy ourselves through our love pain."

Let the nuddy-pants bison disco inferno dance commence!

Tuesday May 24th
Poolside
1:00 p.m.

The olds are all in their swimming cozzies drinking cocktails. Libby has made Our Lord Sandra a sarong. She seems to have forgotten about the cat-plane fandango because she is so spoiled by everyone she meets. If she eats any more I fear an explosion in the knicker department.

Vati is still being ridiculous about my gun.

When I asked him to get me one like in *Thelma and Louise*, he said, "What part of 'not a hope in hell' don't you understand, Georgia?"

"I only want a small one, just for the comedy value of it falling out of my handbag in a café or something. It could even be one of those cigarette lighter things."

But oh no, he is just too busy chatting bollocks to Uncle Eddie about clown cars and beards. Apparently there are more clown cars at the convention than anywhere else in the world.

Vati said, "What a sight: Robin Reliants for as far as the eye could see."

I said, "Hurrah" in an ironic way, but he didn't get it.

Uncle Eddie is allowed to wear his comedy-arrow-through-the-head hat when we go out to dinner.

It is soooo unfair.

Evening

When we were in the Live to Rock diner this huge bloke came over, also wearing a comedy arrow through the head. I thought he was one of Uncle Eddie's sad clown-car mates, but he turned out to be the waiter.

I said, "Could I have a glass of Coca Cola please?"

He said, "Coming right up, ma'am."

I said to Jas, "I could get used to this ma'am business; it makes me feel like Her Maj."

As we were leaving the diner the same bloke brought me this mag called *Dallas Monthly*.

He said, "I thought you would like it because of the cover, ma'am." And the cover was of some heavily-bearded bloke dressed as Her Maj smoking a cigar.

I just said, "Thank you. What a lovely gift."

Wednesday May 25th
Midday

I tried one more time in the phone booth of love, but after speaking to a petrol pump attendant and the mother of twins called Apple and Spaceboy, I decided enough is enough.

On the plus side, we did have a hoot and a half at Graceland, where Elvis the Pelvis lived. And died as it turns out – of a hamburger overdose.

We saw his bedroom and everything, and even his grave. Bought some marvy gifts in the gift emporium for the chums: a lovely Elvis mug, which I am sure some fool (Grandad) will cherish; hilarious wigs, and just to show that we can all live in peace and harmony, I bought the Prat Poodles two Elvis dog outfits. One was a little lurex all-in-one suit from Elvis's Las Vegas days – it even had a doggy-size quiff. The other suit was based on this film called

Jailhouse Rock and was a doggy prisoner outfit with a striped hat. I would have bought Angus and Gordy one each too, but they would have eaten them in minutes. Oh, and I also bought a very elderly man's CD. That was a bit of a mistake actually. This old bloke was sitting in the shop dressed entirely in blue Lurex and humming. I thought he was another elderly Elvis impersonator, but then his "assistant" informed me he was a blues legend.

Jas thought the man said "blue" not "blues". "Why is he a blue legend – does he always wear blue?"

She can be incredibly dim. He was called Moaning Clyde or Wailing Clyde or something – anyway, some kind of complaining was going on namewise. Sadly, Moaning Clyde took a shine to me and kept patting my head, so in desperation I had to buy his CD. And then he made us get a photo taken with him. He was quite a tiny chap and his head was practically resting on one of my nunga-nungas.

Jas whispered to me, "Moaning Clyde is your new boyfriend. He luuurves you."

She might be right, for all I know. I couldn't make out what he was saying; we may be married, for all I know. Still, as I said to Jas, "I don't think a hundred-year age difference is necessarily a barrier to our happiness. The fact that I will never see him again probably is though."

In our hotel
8:00 p.m.
Alone!!!

Dad and Uncle Eddie and Mum and Libby are all at the clown-car evening do with their incredibly sad new mates.

There are twenty-two stations on the TV, which is in a chest of drawers. There isn't a TV in the wardrobe, which is a bit of a blow. But ho hum, pig's bum.

Tuning into the local stations. Mostly it's fools plucking away on banjos and singing "I am the son of a preacher man". Or something about God or grits etc. But then we found a programme with a sort of agony-aunt person. She is called Delilah and is supposed to be cheering people up when they phone in with "luuurve trouble".

She wouldn't have cheered me up, I can tell you that. She was an alarming shade of orange and dressed entirely in pink. There was a suggestion of the criminally insane around the pigtails area. Some poor sod phoned in about her second marriage. She said, "Good evening, Delilah, I'm getting remarried and my son from my first marriage is having a little trouble coming to terms with my wedding. In fact, he is refusing to come. How can I persuade him to enjoy my lovely day?"

Delilah (looking intently into the camera with a mad/concerned look on her face) said, "So what you are saying is that your son is DEVASTATED by your new marriage?"

"Well, I wouldn't say devastated, I would—"

Delilah hadn't finished. "He is MORTIFIED that you have taken another man to YOUR BED who is not his father."

"Well, he hasn't mentioned the bed, it was just that he—"

"He CANNOT BELIEVE his own MOTHER would deceive him and LET HIM DOWN SOOOOO BADLY. He is in TORMENT!"

After having reduced the caller practically to suicide, Delilah then said, "But as you all know, music soothes the troubled breast, and here's a little tune for you to heal the wounds."

♥ 145

The tune was called, "You are a drunk and an unfit mother".

I wanted to ring the helpline number to complain about my mutti and vati, but then I would have only got through to Dad, and he's not even in.

Thursday May 26th
only three days till we go back to England
Poolside

Even if I can't find Masimo I can concentrate on becoming brown as a bee in a bikini. Jas and I had just settled down to heavy sunbathing duties when Vati tried to make us go to the clown-car convention with them.

He said, "What is the point in coming to a new country and then just lolling about by the pool. You could do that anywhere. You should get out and experience the culture."

I said, "Dad, how many hamburgers can one person eat? And anyway, Jas and I are soaking up the culture conversationwise poolsidewise. So get real and cut me some slack here because I am sooooo OVER you."

"Why are you talking rubbish?"

"Well hellOOOO, Dad, do not even GO there – that is

not rubbish, that is Hamburgese."

He went raving and grumbling on, but at last they left me and Jas in peace for a few hours.

3:00 p.m.

I said to Jas, "Have I got strap marks?"

"Let's see... yes, you have."

Excellent!

Evening

In the old Laughter Wagon again on our way to a hotel that everyone has been rambling on about. It's called Gaylords, which says it all in my book.

I said meaningfully to Uncle Eddie and Vati, "You two are certainly in the right place then."

Gaylords is "the Wild West experience under one roof". Apparently people can't be arsed to go to the real West, so they just come to this hotel. We went in through the "saloon door".

Inside Gaylords

Oh, this is so much worse than you can possibly imagine.

There are canyons and waterfalls and deserts all inside a hotel, and everyone is dressed in cowboy outfits, or shorts with high heels and gold belts for the ladeez. (Didn't you know that in the Wild West the ladies wore shorts and high heels?)

I said to Dad, "Now can I have a gun?"

But he and Uncle Eddie were too busy yelling, "Yee-hah" and staggering around in tight leather jeans. Yes, they were wearing tight leather jeans. I will just leave that image with you. Jas and I tried at all times not to be behind them, because then we would have to look at their bottoms bursting out of tight leather jeans.

Erlack.

By the Dodge City cinema there is actually a shop that sells "overalls".

I am not kidding.

Five minutes later
Oh good, Dad and Uncle Eddie have bought some and they have slipped off to the "rest rooms" or "bucks' room" (I know, I know) and come back wearing them.

This is a nightmare scenario.

In the bar area comfort zone they have bucking broncos as bar stools.

Nothing will make me go on one.

Two minutes later

I am sitting on a bucking-bronco stool, I have a pair of horns in between my legs... so has everyone. We are all sitting at the bar on bucking-bronco stools. My dad and Uncle Eddie are wearing overalls. The bar staff are all dressed like Wyatt Earp and crack a whip when you order a drink.

Nothing could be worse.

Wrong. Oh, so very wrongey wrong wrong.

The bucking-bronco bar stools actually buck. I found this out when "Rawhide" came on the speaker system. I was too late getting off, and before I knew it I was being thrown backwards and forwards and round and round. I was clinging on to the horns for dear life. Jas had fallen half off hers and was nearly upside down. Libby was absolutely hooting with laughter and yelling, "Giddyup!!!"

God I feel sick.

The stools eventually stopped bucking when "Rawhide"

finished, and Jas and me scrambled off and had a rest on a rock.

Four minutes later

"Rawhide" came on again, and Libby and Mum, Dad and Uncle Eddie, and everyone else at the bar started bucking about like loonies. It is sooooo sad.

Dad fell off.

Good.

Two minutes later

Dad and Uncle Eddie have made loads of new fat overally mates.

Hoorah.

The fun just goes on and on. From the safety of our rock we were watching a boy with alarmingly big white teeth and those leather things that cowboys wear over their jeans. They are called "chaps" for some reason. Cowboys wear them when they're rounding up cattle. White-teeth Boy wasn't rounding up cattle, he was line dancing like a fool.

I said to Jas, "He makes Sven seem normal."

Then he caught me staring at him, winked and came over.

"Do you mind if I take a little rest beside you, ma'am? I'm a bit saddle sore."

I said, "Sadly, it's a free country."

He sat down and said, "Hi, you all. Whereabouts in Australia are you all from?"

I said, "I'm English."

And he whistled and said, "Awesome!"

Is it?

Then he tipped his hat back and said, "Honey, I bet you are a real good kisser."

What a cheek!

I said with haughtiology and glaciosity, "I'm afraid I don't do snogging with strangers."

Jas almost choked on her mega-size Coca Cola (i.e., Coke in a bucket).

White-teeth Boy said, "What is snoggling?"

Snoggling?

It turned out that Mr Goofy knew next to nothing about the British language. For instance, when I asked politely, "Were you always an arse and a prat, or were you once just a prat?" he didn't understand what I meant.

Fortunately we were interrupted in our interesting

cross-cultural chat by Libby. She came over singing, "Head 'em cup, knead 'em in. Sooooorrreee hide!" and sat on my lap.

She was looking at my new "friend" and then looking at his trousers.

"Georgeee, why is that man so bulgy?"

Then she slipped down from my knee, and before I could stop her she went and stood looking and looking at his pouch trousers. He just had time to say, "Well, how are you all doing, little miss?" Before she thumped him in the trouser-snake area.

Happy days.

And lovely holiday moments.

Friday May 27th
only two more days to go

We were driving to the clown-car convention when we saw a big four-wheel-drive car thing, and in the rear window it had a sticker that said, "Honk if you see the twins fall out," which I though was vair vair *amusant*.

I said to Vati, "We could have one that says, "Don't honk if Uncle Eddie falls out."

Mum said, "Don't be so rude." But she needn't have bothered, as Uncle Eddie had his headphones on and was singing along (badly) to "I am proud to be a redneck". Which I think is spookily karmic, as his whole head is practically now a red neck, if you see what I mean.

At the clown-car convention

In Davy Crockett's diner we were all given fur hats to wear as we ate. Which is nice (ish).

Our alarmingly cheerful waitress came bounding up to us to tell us about the "special".

"Hi there, folks! Todays special has fresh 'erbs, including BAYzil , oRRRREgano, and fresh VEG-a-tables in it."

I said, "Does it come in alUUUUminum foil?"

And me and Jas laughed like drains.

But the waitress didn't get it.

2:00 p.m.

Jas and I slipped off by ourselves to get away from the overall-wearing fools. And do more sunbathing.

Libby came with us to the ice-cream stall and she started her usual shouting. "Me want a big big one pleeeeeeease!"

The elderly man and woman behind us, both dressed from top to toe in gingham, said, "Isn't she the cute one?"

I looked around, but amazingly they were talking about Libby.

"Hey now, let us get you a treat, little lady."

And they paid for her ice cream.

She said, "Fank oo ladies."

They were keen as mustard to know us, and Gingham Man said to me, "How are you all enjoying your day?"

I said, "Oh, fab, I haven't enjoyed myself this much since I injured my ankle playing hockey." But I said it with a charming and light smile.

Mrs Gingham said, "Oh, that is a cute accent you've got there. Whereabouts in Ireland are you from?"

Then Libby, in between mouthfuls of ice cream, said, "I can sing my song."

Oh no. I tried to gag her but she bit my hand and went on really loudly and with gusto. "Poo pooo bum bum. Poo bummy bum bum, arse."

Oh good.

The Ginghams clapped and laughed.

"Oh, soooo cute. But what is "arse"? That is not a word I

know. Is it an Oirish word?"

Libby started smacking her behind, singing, "Bum bum, arse arse." And the Ginghams clapped along. I hope they weren't escapees from the circus-clown-car mental home.

Then Mrs Gingham said, "Oh, I see, honey. You mean your *derrière*! You say arse in Oireland, but in the United States we would say FANNY. Can you say that word, dear? Fanny? Let me pat your little fanny."

I dragged Libby away quickly. With a bit of luck she would forget all about the fanny business.

As we went off, Mrs Gingham yelled, "Now you all come back and visit us from Oireland again, begorrah!"

Good grief.

But God bless them – if you can't beat them, join them, I say.

Jas and I shouted back, "Top of the morning to you!"

Saturday May 28th
Last whole day

The week has whizzed by, even though I didn't have any luck finding Masimo. What I like most about here is that

155

everyone likes us. A LOT. It has made me and Jazzy Spazzy in such a good mood that we even went to watch a clown-car race.

Actually, it has to said that seeing a lot of clown cars roaring around a race track is very hilarious. It's like watching very old people with ponytails skating or something. At least my dad doesn't do that.

Dad and Mum and Uncle Eddie have made loads of new mates, and we all went out to a takeaway hamburger place for the last lunch. You drive up to some clown-head thing and then you shout your order at it and it talks back to you and then you go and get your order. Now that is what I call culture. Why can't we have something like that in England? I think I'll suggest it to Hawkeye when I get back to Stalag 14. It would make lunchtime a whole new experience clown-head thingwise.

Nuddy-pants bison-horn photo session

As the olds went off to get last-minute pressies and Libby went to get something for the kitties, Jas and I made our small but meaningful tribute to our visit to Hamburger-a-gogo land.

The only good thing about the nightmare trip to Gaylords was that me and Jas got to buy some souvenir bison-horn hats. So we were able to wear them for our farewell nuddy-pants photo session in the hotel room.

It was vair vair amusing. Jas in the nuddy-pants and bison horns reading a book on the ginormous bed. Me adjusting the TV in the bathroom in my bison horns and nuddy-pants. Packing suitcases, applying lippy, etc. Vair vair amusing indeed. I was nearly dead with laughing.

Sunday May 29th
Farewell Hamburger-a-gogo

Loreen and Jolene and Noelene and Gaylene and all the other "lenes" at the hotel actually cried when we left... honestly. They were hugging us and so on, saying, "Now, you all come back to us, soon as you can, missing you already."

Still, as I said to Jas, they are only human.

Adios amigos, as you say in Hamburger-a-gogo land. I love you all. But I must go as I have a Luuurve God to find.

Bum bum bum bum oley bum bum, and good afternoon officer

Still Sunday May 29th
Circling over England
7:45 p.m.
Blimey it looks like toytown.

Heathrow Airport
Home again, home again, jiggity jig!

Rain rain, lovely rain.

Vati's ludicrous van mate has come to pick us up. His van has a big sticker on it that says, "If you are looking for love, have a look at the driver's horn."

Still, no one knows me at Heathrow.

8:30 p.m.

As we were trying to get all our stuff in the van, a policeman came to tell us to move along because we were blocking the road.

I beamed at him. "Good morrow, constable, and how are you on this fine English eve?"

He looked at me as rain bounced off his helmet. "I'm as well as can be expected under the circumstances, madam."

"We've just come back from Hamburger-a-gogo land and the police over there have guns. Do you have a gun concealed about your person, officer?"

"I very often wish I did, madam. Can you pop into your van now so that we can sort out the twelve-mile tailback you're causing?"

Mum said, "I honestly am doing my best, sergeant, but my husband's comedy cowboy hat is a bit difficult to fit in anywhere without..."

I could see that the officer was on the point of violently shoving Mum and the hat in the back of the van, when Libby piped up. "I know a song, Mr Bobbyman."

Even I have to admit that Bibs can look like an ordinary charming child sometimes, and she had her fairy crown on and a pink dress, so you could be forgiven for the mistake.

The officer sighed and bent down to her. "OK, just sing me a little verse before your mummy and daddy quickly get in the van and GO HOME."

You never know what toddlers will remember. Libby sang her botty song to the officer. But worse, much worse than that, she sang the American version. She put her hands on her hips and gave her all to the constable.

"Bum oley, bum oley, fanny fanny bum bum."

I thought he was going to faint. He tried to stop her – God knows we all did – but on it went, even when Dad put her under his arm and shoved her in the back of the van.

"Poo poo and bummy bum bum FANNY! Pat my little fanny!!!"

9:00 p.m.

Dropped Jazzy Spazzy off at her house. She said, "It'll be weird not being together, won't it? Call me as soon as you get home."

I very nearly hugged her. But then I remembered we are back in Stiff Upper Lip land and I don't want any rumours of lesbianism to spread; you never know who might be watching.

On the way home to our house we sang "I was born under a wandering star". Vati is in a remarkably good mood. I can't believe that looking at clown cars can cheer you up, but it has.

Mum is still full of herself because all the men across "the pond" called her "ma'am".

Still, it was nice of them to take me and Jas to Hamburger-a-gogo, even if I didn't manage to find the Luuurve God.

Of course, the plus side is that now we are back, I don't need to see anything of them. I will be out all night and all day with my boyfriend.

If I've got a boyfriend.

I don't even know if he's back yet.

Oh, hello... Welcome back to the rack of love.

We arrived at our gate and unpacked all our luggage. The van man and Uncle Eddie drove off with a squeal of tyres. Uncle Eddie, still wearing his comedy arrow through the head, yelled, "Head 'em up, ride 'em out, RAWHIIIIIDE. Yeee-haaah!"

I saw Mr Next Door bob down underneath his window so that we couldn't see him. I also noticed that the anti-cat fence has been taken down. He will be thrilled with our Prat outfits. I may take them round later when he thinks we've gone to bed.

9:15 p.m.
Home! Our lovely house, surprisingly not a burned-out wreck.

Happy days.

I even found myself hugging Grandad.

No sign of his girlfriend.

In the loo
Ermmm... wrong about there being no sign of Maisie.

I am not being ungrateful, but why would anyone normal knit a toilet-seat cover?

In the Kitchen
Or knit covers for the door handles?

No sign of the kittykats.

Mum and Dad and Libby have taken Grandvati home, so it's just me in the same bat place.

I am going to think about all my experiences and what I

have learned on my great adventure about life, love and the universe.

I am simply going to enjoy my own mind.

In the peace and tranquility of my own room.

The simple joy of just being alone with my own deep inner thoughts.

In my bedroom

Please tell me it's not true that I am now the proud owner of knitted slippers.

9:20 p.m.

Rang Jas.

"Jas."

"Howdy."

"Howdy, how are you all doing?"

"Just fine and how are you all?"

"Have you heard anything from anyone?"

"There were about ten messages from Tom. He's having a nice time and everything, but he really misses me, and oh, he mentioned—"

"Jas, pleased though I am for your news about wombats

and so on, what I want to know is have you heard anything, you know, from the gang or anything?"

"Georgia, I have only been in the house for twenty minutes."

9:22 p.m.
Phoned Rosie.

Rosie's mum answered the phone.

I said, "Is Rosie in?"

"I'm afraid not, dear. She's gone to homework club."

Homework club?

Oh, yes, the old homework-club scenario – it's the Ace Gang code for going somewhere you're not allowed to. In Ro Ro's case it will be Sven's snogging emporium.

Tried Jools.

Out at homework club.

Ditto Ellen and Mabs.

Crikey! I hope they've not formed a lesbian coven.

Phoned Jas back.

"The Ace Gang are all out at homework club. What does that mean?"

"Perhaps they are, you know, doing their homework."

"Jas, are you mad?"

Hummmph.

Back from a million years abroad and the Ace Gang can't even be bothered to say "welcome home".

Back to Stalag 14 tomorrow.

I feel a bit sheer desperadoes because nothing has changed. No one has got in touch so I don't know where Masimo is. Is he back? Perhaps he has decided to stay over in Hamburger-a-gogo.

Oh *merde*.

Even the kittykats are all out – no sign of them anywhere. Once again I have dropped anchor in Poo Bay.

9:30 p.m.

Went round to Mr and Mrs Next Door's. I am sure they saw me coming up their drive and pretended to be out; I heard a muffled bark from inside the house. They are vair vair nervous people. Still, live and let die, I say, and I posted the Prat brothers' Elvis outfits through the letterbox.

I am sure they will love them a lot.

Really I am too good for this world.

Oscar, Mr and Mrs Across the Road's prepubescent, sex-maniac son, was on perve duty on the wall as I went back into my house. He looked across at me as I passed and said, "Cracking tits."

Oh, lovely.

10:00 p.m.

You always hear people moaning on about jet lag, don't you? "Oooh, I had to go straight to bed, I didn't feel right for three weeks." Namby-pambies. It's just another form of trave... zzzzzzzzzzzzzzz.

Monday May 30th

7:30 a.m.

What happened? Did someone creep into my room with a mallet? I feel appalling. No one could expect me to go to school. I'll just snuggle down and... Hang on a minute! How will I find out about Masimo if I don't go out? I must be brave for my love.

Still no sign of the kittykats. I know they've been around, though, because all the plants are just stumps.

8:30 a.m.

Met Jas. She looked like death warmed up. She said, "God, I'm tired. Are you?"

I said, "Not many, Benny. Still, we can have an afternoon nap during German."

Stalag 14

When Jas and me got to the school gates the Ace Gang were waiting for us. We had a celebratory Klingon greeting and a quick burst of disco inferno. I felt quite emotional and came over all American. I hugged Rosie, I was so pleased to see her. She shoved me off and said, "Get off me, you appalling tart. And I mean that in a loving way."

Oh, it's so good to get back to normal.

Behind the fives court
Break time

Rosie said, "So what happened? Did you find Masimo?"

I said, "Well, in the end I thought, you know, it was a bit, like, uncool to get in touch, so I—"

Jas said, "So she phoned up all these complete strangers and made an idiot of herself instead."

Oh, thank you, Mrs What a Great Pal. NOT.

Actually, the gang were really nice about it. Jools said, "Well, he doesn't know you tried to find him, so he can go on thinking you are full of glaciosity."

And Ellen, for once, said something quite sensible. "And you are quite brown."

Good point, actually.

They wanted to hear everything about our trip, so we treated them to a quick chorus from Delilah's song "You are a drunk and unfit mother" and then told them all about Hamburger-a-gogo. You know – all about the different culture and the chance to communicate with foreign people in their own language.

Rosie said, "Let me get this right. You went to a place that was actually called Gaylords? And you rode a bucking-bronco bar stool?"

"Yes."

"With horns?"

"Yes."

"Please say you took photos."

Jas said, "Better than that. We brought you all special replica horns to wear. Look."

She got the gift horns out of her rukky and the Ace Gang tried them on.

They were thrilled, going "Oh wow!!!" and "Fabarooney!!!"

They looked *magnifique*.

Jools said, "We should form a band called the Bisons."

11:15 a.m.

The American disco inferno bison dance is born.

It is: foot stomp, foot stomp, arse wiggle.

Horns to the right, horns to the left, and clap.

Foot stomp, foot stomp, arse wiggle.

Horns to the right, horns to the left, and clap!

Ellen said, "It's like good and everything, but bisons don't clap, do they?"

Good grief. If it was up to people like Ellen, *The Simpsons* might never exist. She'd be saying, "No one has blue hair two feet high" and other gibberish.

I said, "That is where you are vair vair wrong, Ellen. Out on the range, when a travelling circus pulls in, the bison and the rest of the prairie folk go to see it, and the biggest clappers are always the bison."

Ellen looked even more confused than normal. I said,

"Ellen, of course they don't clap, but neither do they do disco dancing. It's poetic whatsit, you steaming ninny."

As we loped into Stalag 14 past the prison warders, Wet Lindsay and Hawkeye, and their guard dog, Astonishingly Dim Monica, Mabs said, "So you don't know where Masimo is?"

I said, "No, I don't know whether he's back or what's happening."

Wet Lindsay glared at me as we went in. I think she may have lost weight while I've been away. It's not a good look unless you like looking like a vair vair thin twit.

4:30 p.m.

Bloody *sacré bleu*. We've had our bison horns confiscated! How are we supposed to form a band now?

I was grumbling to Jas as we slouched off home. "Honestly, how petty is this place? I KNEW Wet Lindsay would try something. She's got it in for me."

Jas said, "We should have taken them off after German."

"Where is the law that says bison horns shall not be worn in the school corridors? Tell me that. Where is that law written down?"

"You said that to Wet Lindsay."

"I know I did, Jas. I was there."

"She said, 'Don't be ridiculous, there is no law written down that says don't poo in the corridors, but we know not to do it.'"

"I know she did and I think it's disgusting that we have to put up with that sort of language – poo talk – from supposed Head Girls."

"You said that to her as well."

"JAS, I KNOW I said that to her. I was there!!!"

"That's when she gave us all bad conduct marks."

"Yes, well, that is typico."

Home

I HATE Stalag 14. They treat us like bloody children. I wanted to practise my bison dance.

6:00 p.m.

Mabs phoned. "Gee, I bumped into Dom and he asked if we're going to the Stiff Dylans gig next weekend."

"Wowzee wow! Did you ask him about Masimo?"

"Er, no, I thought that would be uncool."

"Good thinking, Batwoman."

It is good thinking, but annoying, too, as I don't know anything about the Luuurve God.

On the brighter side, there is a Stiff Dylans gig, so if nothing else it means that Masimo will be back by then.

Tuesday May 31st
English

Still no news of Masimo. I was asking the Ace Gang what I should do but Miss Wilson kept interrupting our chat with her so-called "love of Shakespeare". For goodness' sake. Hers is not the love that dares not speak its name – hers is the love that bangs on and on about Billy. It's all "What ho, my lord" and "Oh look, here comes Macbeth talking total bollocks." On the plus side, she reminded us that the Foxwood lads are coming to help us backstage (oo-er) when we rehearse.

Wednesday June 1st
8:15 a.m.

Something really really freaky-deaky and weird happened. The doorbell rang and everyone had already gone out so I answered it and it was the postman. He said to me, "I have

172

a registered parcel for Miss Georgia Nicolson. Is she in?"

I said, "Oh, come on, you know I'm in, you're talking to me."

He's a surly old bugger. He shouldn't really have a job with the public, unless it's the public that lives in a prison. He said in his surly, officious way, "Well, you say that, Miss, but have you any way of identifying yourself?"

Now he was really getting on my nerves. I was just about to rip the parcel out of his hands when I had a vair vair amusing idea. I said, "A way of identifying myself? Yes, I believe I have. Would you just wait a moment?"

I came back a minute later with a mirror, looked into it and said, "Yep, it is definitely me."

8:30 a.m.
In the end he handed over the parcel.

Hmmm, what was the postmark?

Oh. New Zealand. If Tom has sent me a copy of "You're the only fish in my sea" or some photos of wombat snot, I may go mad.

It wasn't from Tom.

It was a letter from the Sex God. Robbie.

173

Blimey O'Reilly's panties.

I had a really queasy feeling as I began to read what it said.

Dear Georgia,

It's been a while since I wrote. I suppose I thought that you would reply and then I would write again. But you didn't, so... Tom arrived last week and it was brilliant to see him. We've been out in the bush... ·

I was thinking, *Oh here we go – back to hugging wombats and plucking guitars in the river,* but no...

...talking about home, and talking about you actually.

Tom told me about the boy-entrancer episode and your excellent dancing to "Three little boys". I thought I would never stop laughing. But it made me sad, too, because you like someone else and also because I'm quite a serious person and you are, in the nicest possible way, quite possibly clinically insane, and at the very least, a handful. I can just hear you saying oo-er to that last bit.

I don't know why I am writing, really. I suppose I wanted

you to have a picture of me out here, which I have enclosed, and I would really like one of you sometime.

You are always in my heart and often in my dreams.

Robbie

xxxxx

Oh God.

The photo was of him in jeans and a T-shirt sitting by a river. He was looking straight into the camera with those deep blue-black eyes that I thought I would never ever be able to look at again. He was just so... oh, I don't know.

8:45 a.m.

Got to Jas in a state of shock.

She was rambling on as usual. "Come on, come on, we'll be late. What's wrong with you? You look like you've seen a ghost. Anyway, Tom phoned last night, he said they found this amazing mushroom that was about two feet across. It's apparently delicious if you—"

"Jas, I... I..."

"And he said, do you know what, the Maoris eat the

175

larvae of the Hu Hu bug, they are big fat white grubs, and they roast them and then they eat them. Tom went to a hangi out there, he has a new Maori friend and his traditional Maori name is Brian and—"

"Jas, look at this."

Jas took the letter as we jogged along. And even she was silent.

She finished it and then looked at me.

"Bugger my giddy aunt."

For once Jas is not exaggerating.

I just don't know what to think. I had given up on the Sex God. I really had.

French

I kept looking at his photo.

He was bloody gorgey. And I mean that most sincerely.

But what in the name of Jas's commodious botty huggers was I supposed to do or think? He hadn't said, "Come to Kiwi-a-gogo and be mine." Nor had he said, "I am coming home to get you." In fact, to be frank, what he had said really was, "I still like you and think about you a bit."

Oh, why hadn't he written this last month? Why had he

written it after another Luuurve God had come along?

It's too much.

Break

I consulted with the Ace Gang.

They listened while Jas read the letter out loud. I don't know why I let her because she read it soooo badly, with a really crap New Zealand accent for some reason. I can safely say I am not optimistic that her performance of Lady Macbeth is going to bring the house down.

Then they all started the insane nodding-dog extravaganza.

I said, "So what do you think?"

Rosie said, "Dump him from your mind. He is yesterday's snoggee; move on, move up. We've gone European now, we are Euro citizens and it is our duty to kop off with as many European types as we can. Within reason."

Jools said, "On the other hand he is very very groovy-looking."

Mabs said, "And it would be quite nice to be Jas's sister-in-law, wouldn't it?"

Blimey O'Reilly's knob, I hadn't thought of that nightmare scenario.

Jas almost choked on her nibbly niblets.

It was, as ever, left to Ellen to completely and utterly confuse humanity. She said, "Well, I suppose... like really, you are, like, well... not really anyone's girlfriend."

Home
6:30 p.m.
I'd ask Mum for advice but you might as well ask Angus, for all the sense she makes. And also, she has gone out with Dad and Libby to the O'Shaunesseys' to show them our holiday photos.

8:00 p.m.
I wish I could talk to someone normal. Or even in.

Even the kittykats are out. Gordy is worse than his dad. He sleeps all day, wakes up, eats anything he sees, destroys a bit of furniture or some tights and then buggers off out. They both treat this house like a furry hotel.

10:30 p.m.
I can't believe this. Mum and Dad have come back Irish. We are being forced to be an Irish family. Vati says he has

rediscovered his Irish roots.

I said, "Yes, after six pints of Guinness."

He wouldn't shut up, though, and put on a Dubliners record. Libby is doing her version of Irish dancing. I don't remember the knickerless part, but...

In between slapping his thighs and shouting, "Come on there, girl, get them pegs moving!!" he said, "You see, there is a story in my family that my great-great-grandfather was an O'Dwyer from Killarney, but they changed the family name to protect them against the villainous English."

I said, "Dad, when you say villainous English, do you mean us?"

But he wouldn't be stopped. "They changed the name to Nicolson."

I said, "What, that grand old English name? NOT. Why would they change their name from an Irish one to a Scottish one? The English, i.e., us, hated the Och Aye landers just as much as the Leprechaun-a-gogo folk. More. That is why we built Hadrian's wall at the top of England – to keep the Ginger beardey folk out."

Dad was still rambling on like Paddy O'Mad. "And another thing: we look Irish. That man in Memphis spotted it – he asked you if you were Irish. He asked you that because you have the look of the Emerald Isle about you."

"No, he didn't, Dad. He was an American – he doesn't know where anyone comes from unless it's Texas. He was wearing gingham."

I slammed up to my bedroom.

Bed of pain

Ohgodohgodohgod.

I lay on my bed with a pillow over my head.

I am in a ditherosity of love and I have now become Oirish.

Thursday June 2nd

Jas got top marks again in history. She went all red and girlish.

As we walked home I said to her, "You are vair clever, Jazzy. You are as clever as Professor Clever at the University of Oxford department of Cleverosity."

I feel a bit better about the whole Robbie thing. If I don't mention his name, then I won't think about him. It's like voodoo, isn't it?

It is definitely beyond the Valley of Deffo and entering the Vale of Very Nearly Quite Sure that I luuurve Masimo.

Bathroom
4:45 p.m.
I checked the orang-utan situation. You can practically comb my legs.

4:48 p.m.
I can't be bothered with using Immac. Actually, what I mean is that Mum has run out.

4:50 p.m.
Dad has got one of those razors that leaves your skin smoothy smooth and attractive to women. So it says on the TV ad. I do want smoothy-smooth skin but I don't want to be attractive to women.

5:00 p.m.
I could risk it on my legs. What sensible lesbian is going to be at knee level with me?

5:01 p.m.

I won't think about the possibility of midget lesbians that are only one foot high.

5:45 p.m.

Actually, Dad's razor is really tip-top. I have no open gashes at all and my legs are like the advert says – smoothy smooth.

Mmmmmmmmm.

Washed the soap off Dad's razor and put it back where it was.

In my room
7:00 p.m.

Now then, the age-old question of what to wear for the Stiff Dylans gig. I must of course wear a short skirt to show off the smoothy smoothness of my legs. I would be a fool to waste the smoothy smoothnosity.

7:30 p.m.

I think if I'm wearing a really short skirt, I should wear a more covery-up top so that the nungas are not on display. I want to hint at sophisticosity, not prostitutenosity.

8:00 p.m.

I was just trying things on when my father went mad – yelling and barging about downstairs. I think I might tell him that swearing is an indication of lack of vocabulary. But not just now.

8:10 p.m.

He barged into my room, his face covered in bits of loo paper. Is this his new Irish look? He yelled, "Did you use my bloody razor?"

I looked hurt and puzzled.

"Your razor? I know this is your first shot at fatherhood, but perhaps you have noticed I am a girl. I am beardless. Mostly."

He said, "Don't be so bloody cheeky, you know damn well what I mean. HAVE you been using my razor?"

"Well, only a bit, just for my, you know, legs."

Why do I have to discuss my body with my father? I am sure there's a law about it.

Fifty years later, after his famous lecture about not using his stupid razor ever again, he went off.

8:30 p.m.
Shame about his face being all cut.

8:40 p.m.
Still... nice smoothy-smooth legs.

Friday June 3rd
8:15 a.m.
There is a certain amount of tensionosity about not knowing whether the Luuurve God is back in the country. I had relaxed my make-up regime because he was not around, and now I have to be on high alert all the time just in case. Also, and I know this is even for me bordering on the Universe of Madnosity, now that I have heard from Robbie, I sort of have to wear make-up all the time because I've got a letter from him, which has put him in my head and that might mean he can see me. From my head. Or from his letter. I told you I have entered the Valley of the Unwell. Get out of my head, ex Sex God!!!

I am going to try a bit of nostril breathing even at the risk of expanded nostrils.

Aaaaahhhhhh.

Four minutes later

I am a xxxxxx-free zone and I think you know that the xxxxxx starts with an R.

Donner and Blitzen and also *schiessenhausen*!!! I've thought of him again.

Make-up plan

My routine is a bit of lippy and gloss with a hint of mascara and just a really tiny bit of eyeliner. The difficulty is getting past sniffer-dog Hawkeye. Today I will be returning to that old favourite of putting my head as far into my bag as it will go and saying as I go past Hawkeye, "Oh, now where did I put my French homework? *Mon Dieu* and *Au secours,* it must be in here somewhere."

Ambling up the hill to Stalag 14

Jas said, "Did you reply to Robbie?"

Oh God.

"Er... no."

"Are you going to?"

"I don't know, Jas."

"Well, you used to really like him and he has written to

♡ 185

you, so are you going to reply or not?"

I didn't say anything so she just went on. "And if you do reply what will you say?"

I still didn't reply.

"I mean, are you going to talk to Tom about it when he gets back and ask his advice? He's back next week, you know, so will you wait until then and reply, or what?"

Eventually I was driven to having to reply to her. "Jas, shouldn't you be wearing a doublet and a false moustache and burning me at a stake? You are quite literally the Spanish Inquisition."

"Well, I am just saying..."

"Well, don't."

"Usually you want to go on and on about Robbie and Masimo, your so-called boyfriends."

"Jas, don't start... and anyway, you're having a laugh, aren't you? If I go on about MY boyfriends all the time, how come I know all the words to 'You are the only fish in my sea'? How come?"

Jas got the hump. "Oh, well, I'm sorry to bother you with MY life! Of course YOUR life is the only important thing, isn't it? Yes, yes, Georgia Nicolson is the only person in the universe. Not."

And she stalked off like a stalking stalker at a stalking contest.

Blimey, she could get huffy.

Ah well, I might try my Oirish charm on her, when I can be bothered.

Geoggers

Jas kept up her cold shoulders all morning, even when I sent her a little gift of two pieces of chocolate. She ate them and then went on *ignorez-vous*ing me!

Break

Jools was telling us the latest about her and Rollo. They have been to an all-nighter and spent the whole night together. She has snogged so much that she's got a cold sore coming on her lip. She showed us all.

Erlack.

Apparently sixteen of them stayed round at this mate of Rollo's while his parents were abroad and snogged the night away.

Ellen, as usual, was a bit baffled. "Did you all, you know, snog at the same time, or... er, was there dancing?"

Mabs said, "So, is Rollo like your bloke now?"

Jools said, "Well, I think so, but I never know when he's going to see me or ring me."

I said, "Blimey! So it's a sort of full-time s'later situation."

Jools said, "Yes, I suppose it is. Like on Saturday, I don't know if he's going to the gig with me or whether he'll turn up there and be with me or..."

Jas said, "I wouldn't stand for that. I need to know where I am."

I said, "You're here, Jas." and I gave her my bestest smile.

She didn't smile back. But she did say, quite nastily, "And who will you be seeing at the gig, Georgia? Or will you be just having a LAUGH, if you know what I mean and I think you do."

Oh God, she is playing dirty now, with this Dave the Laugh thing. She knows that I still haven't told Ellen anything about me and Dave.

School gates
4:20 p.m.

We were all ambling out of the playground when I saw him. Masimo on his scooter. Parked outside the school gates!

188

Ohmygiddygodspyjamas!!! I couldn't believe it was him. But it was!

He is absolutely gorgey. He has a tan as well. His hair is so black and wavy and he's got long legs and a fit body and everything.

He was just sitting on his scooter with his helmet in his lap, leaning back on one arm. He had shades on.

He is sooooo sexy. You could feel like a beam of sexicosity coming off him.

What was he doing here? Was he waiting for me?

The Ace Gang were doing their marvellous impression of walking goldfish.

Rosie said, "My God, he's fit."

Jools said, "Blimey. Did you know he was going to be here?"

Jas said, "He's brown, isn't he? He's browner than you."

I couldn't speak. All the girls streaming out of the gates were looking at him and doing that silly flicky-hair thing and smiling. Shutup smiling, you smiling minxes. I didn't know what to do. Should I just walk casually by him and *ignorez-vous* him, carrying on with my Mystery Woman scenario? Or should I be friendly and nice and smiley? Oh, I don't know.

I dithered around and made the Ace Gang walk really really slowly.

Had I got enough lippy on?

Was I wearing clothes?

I was just saying, "Oh my God ohmygod. What shall I do?" when I was saved from any decision making because Lindsay appeared at the gates. She wasn't wearing her uniform. She had a short white suit on and a headscarf. She went straight up to Masimo, doing a sort of ridiculous little run thing, and kissed him on the cheek!

He was smiling at her, and they were chatting. God, he has a nice smile. He has a really generous, big mouth – not like Mark Big Gob, just normal big. I couldn't help looking and watching like a sort of horror film. Even Jas stopped *ignorez-vous*ing me and linked arms with me because she knew how horrible it was.

We were very near to the gate now and I couldn't avoid going through it and passing by Masimo. The gang sort of shielded me and I kept my head down, but I still saw Lindsay putting on the spare helmet. It was awful. I was so miserable and trudged off with the gang.

I heard the scooter rev up and roar off behind me.

Rosie said, "That was a bit intense."

Everyone was really nice to me. Which sort of made it worse. They kept saying, "Are you all right? Do you want some chuddie?"

But nothing helped.

4:30 P.M.

After they had all peeled off home, it was just me and Jas.

She said, "Blimey O'Reilly, that is a turn up for *le livre*."

I said, "I must be jinxed in love. What have I done in a past life to deserve this?"

Jas said, "Perhaps you were, you know, like a wasp or something."

"A wasp?"

Jas is what is known in the business as an unhelp. But she can't help being a tiny dim pal. At least she's not me, though.

As she went off into her house she gave me a little squeeze on the arm and said, "I don't care what anyone else says about you – I like you."

I MUSTN'T cry. I must not cry until I get into my bedroom.

High Street
4:45 p.m.

Tosser Thompson and his mates passed me and said something, but I didn't know what. I felt like a ghost in the world.

I got to my gate and I could feel the tears welling up in my eyes. No one would be home yet, so at least I could get into bed and just wail.

What a hopeless fool I was.

I had even phoned up people with the same name as him in Manhattan.

One of them was a Chinese takeaway.

That is how pathetic I am.

5:00 p.m.

I was opening the gate when I heard the roar of a scooter coming up my road. I didn't turn around. Even if Dad had got an even more embarrassing vehicle than the clown car, nothing mattered any more.

But then the scooter stopped behind me. And he spoke. Him. In person. Himself. Not a facsimile of a sham. Him. The person I had been dreaming of for so long.

"Georgia, *ciao*, how are you? *Come sta?*"

I couldn't speak. I turned round. And looked at him. I looked straight into his eyes. I had forgotten how amber they were, sort of soft-and-hard-looking at the same time. He half smiled at me, and he has gorgey teeth – let's face it, he's gorgey all over.

"I just stop to say *ciao*. I have been away."

I still couldn't speak. Maybe nodding was all right? I nodded. Oh good, I was being a budgie in a school uniform. Eggscellent. Shutup, brain. You haven't joined in so far, don't start now.

He revved up his engine and said, "I too must go. We are rehearsing. Are you coming to the gig? I hope to see you there. *Ciao*."

Oh dear *Gott* in *Himmel*!!!

6:30 p.m.
Lying on my bed
 I think I might be in a coma.
 I have to speak to someone normal about this.

7:00 p.m.

Can't think of anyone.

7:30 p.m.

Still can't think of anyone.

7:45 p.m.

Gave up on talking to someone normal and called an Ace Gang emergency meeting at Luigi's.

9:30 p.m.

In between slurping coffee, the Ace Gang gave me the pep talk to end all pep talks. I have to go out and get my man!!! Yee-hah!

Rosie even sang the national anthem and said, "Gird your loins and adjust your nungas for battle."

Midnight

I mean, why would he come round to my house to say *ciao* if he didn't like me a bit?

1:00 a.m.

What is it with boys? Just when I thought I'd forgotten about my heartbreakosity *vis à vis* Robbie (*Merde* I've thought of his name again. I am going to have to call him something else so as not to attract the voodoo thing. I will call him... er... the Guitar Plucker.)... Anyway, where was I before I so rudely interrupted myself? Oh yes. Just when I thought I had forgotten about my heartbreakosity *vis à vis* the Guitar Plucker, he sends me a really nice letter. Then Masimo pops by.

Oh, I don't know!!!

Saturday June 4th
Churchill Square
11:00 a.m.

Rosie said, "In this sort of situation, she who dares shops." So in preparation for the Battle of the Chicks I am going to get a fabby and marvy pair of shoes.

Ravel
11:30 a.m.

I saw these cool shoes in the window, with a bit of a kitten heel

♡ 195

and some groovy strappy bits round the toes and the heel.

In the shoe shop
We all trooped in and I asked for my size. The woman said the biggest they had was a size four until next week.

Next week! Is she mad? I have to go the gig, like, tonight!

I said to her, "OK, please bring me them."

Jas said, "What's the point of that, you take a size seven?"

"Sometimes."

Rosie, who was trying on some ludicrous furry boots that made her look like a yeti, said, "So do your feet change size then?"

I said, "Well, you know, it *says* a size seven, but then if they are made in Japan where they have very tiny feet, size seven is like a size fifteen over here."

They all looked at me.

Then the lady with the shoes came back. They were groovy as anything. Masimo would love them because, as every fool knows, Italians are the mistresses of footwear.

Five minutes later
Blimey. I couldn't get my heels in. I said politely to the lady,

"Have you got a horn?"

And that set the gang off into hysterics.

She looked at us like we were loons, but went off to get the shoehorn.

Five minutes later

Got them on! Yesss!!

The lady in the shop said, "Are you sure they fit? Walk around in them."

The gang were all slouched about waiting for me not to be able to walk. I got up. Ouch ouch and double *merde* and ouch. They were bloody aggers. I looked in the mirror. They looked fab. I must have them; I must go through the pain for him. I smiled like a loon. "Do you know, it's amazing, they are sooooo comfy as well as being groovy. It's almost like wearing slippers."

Bedroom

1:00 p.m.

I have stuffed my new shoes with newspapers to try and stretch them.

♡ 197

1:30 p.m.

Mum came snuffling around. "Give us a look at your new shoes."

I said, "Oh, I'll show you later when I'm all dressed up."

5:30 p.m.

Dad said he didn't know anyone who stayed in the bathroom for four hours. It's a great pity that he doesn't spend a lot more time on his appearance.

In my room
5:45 p.m.

I have two mirrors arranged so that I can see back and front. I am so smoothy everywhere that I am like a human billiard ball – there is not one single lurking rogue hair on my entire body. I am a lurker-free zone, and I have at least got my base coat of make-up on.

6:00 p.m.

I've got a couple of jumbo rollers in my hair, which I will take out at the last moment when I've done everything else so that I have max bounceabililty.

6:30 P.M.

Calm, ohm. Save myself and my energy for the battle. Better check the weather. Hmmm, a bit cloudy.

Phoned Jas. "Jas, do you think it will rain?"

Jas said, "Just a min."

I heard her scampering around, and then she came back to the phone.

"No, I think dry spells with just a tiny possibility of precipitation."

Blimey. I had to ask – I knew I shouldn't, but I had to. "Jas, can I ask how you found that out?"

"Oh, yes, well, the snails in the jar that Tom and I placed in the—"

"Jas, I really must dash. Libby is watching *The Sound of Music* again and I need to yodel along. See you at eight."

7:00 P.M.

Just about ready. I am not going to risk the boy entrancers, even though they are fab and entrance boys like billio. I don't want to take any risks gluewise. I've put eight coats of mascara on, so that should do the trick. I put on one coat and then put talcum powder over it and then another coat

♡ 199

and so on. I can hardly lift my top lids up, but I like to think that gives me a mysterious sexualosity.

7:15 p.m.
My little blue skirt looks vair fab and I have put fake tan on my legs to top up my Hamburger-a-gogo browniness. I don't think you can really see the streaky bits unless you're at floor level, and who is going to be there? Apart from the midget lesbians I was worrying about before. I have got my strict bra on, the one that takes no nonsense from my basoomas, and a fabby blue and black top, which has got a really small pair of lips on it down at the bottom. You don't notice it, but if you did, it would imply I liked snogging without implying I am a tart.

7:25 p.m.
Mum called up: "Can I come and see what you're wearing?"

Oh God.

I put my shoes on.

OH my God!!! Ag city Arizona! They were made for a child! I pushed my feet in and managed to get them on. And stood up. If I walked about I would probably get used to them.

Mum came in. "Wow. You look really groovy! Is this for the Italian Stallion?"

Shut up. Please shut up.

Then she noticed my shoes. "Are they your new shoes? They are gorge, aren't they? Aren't they a bit too small for you?"

I said, smiling widely, "Gosh no, if anything they are a bit slack."

She was still looking at them. "What size are they?"

I looked at my watch and said, "Crikey O'Reilly, is that the time? I promised to meet the gang at seven thirty. S'later."

I dashed off down the stairs. Ouch ouch, aggers aggers. Bugger bugger bum.

On the way to Jas's

My God, these shoes hurt. On the plus side I think they're cutting off the blood supply to my feet, so with a bit of luck my feet will be numb soon.

I had to sit up on a wall for a resties just round the corner from Jas's house.

7:45 p.m.

As we walked along Jas said, "Do you want to go to the loo? You're walking funny."

Clock tower
8:00 p.m.

Met up with the Usual Suspects. Rosie had actually bought the furry yeti boots. Maybe they are to match Sven's. He has the most unusual dress sense I have come across in someone who is not actually working in a circus. I wouldn't have thought you could buy shiny purple suits with scarlet inserts, but you can. Also, if I could bear to think about it, I would say that he was wearing lipstick. He lifted me up and kissed me on both cheeks. "Hi, girly girls, let's hit it!!"

I looked into my compact. Yep, he was wearing lipstick.

We all trailed after him.

Jools is in a state of near madnosity about whether she is going out with Rollo or not. Jas is in one of her philosophical moods, so she said to Jools, "If it is meant to be, then it will be. Did I show you my song from Tom called 'You are the only fish in my sea'?"

As Jas got it out (oo-er) to read to Jools, I walked on

quickly with the rest of the gang. Ouch ouch ouchey ouch. Still got feeling in my feet.

Ellen said, "I think I am going to, like, make Dave the Laugh jealous."

I laughed and said, "Oh yeah, good luck."

And she looked at me.

"How do you mean?"

I said, "Well, he, you know he's not, erm... he doesn't really seem like the jealous type, does he?"

Ellen said, "Well, I'm going to, you know, dance and flick my hair about with that friend of Rollo's. I'm going to try all those tricks and stuff."

I said, "Promise me you won't try the infectious laugh."

By this time we were outside the Buddha Lounge.

In the tarts' wardrobe
8:40 p.m.

We had a last-minute Ace Gang conference.

Well, Rosie, Jas and I did. Mabs and Ellen and Jools were so eager for boy action that they did a quick lippy check, visit to the piddly-diddly department and off out on to the disco dance inferno emporium.

203

Rosie said, "Go through the check list."

I sat on the edge of a sink. (Oh, the relief the relief in the tootsies department.)

I began, "Mascara?"

We looked at my mascara. "Check."

"Lippy and lurker situation." Jas and Rosie looked and said together, "Check."

I said, "Attractive smile full of Eastern promise?" And I smiled.

Rosie said, "Phwoar, give us a snog, I've come over all lesbian."

I like to think she was joking.

I am ready to take on Lindsay. Flicky flicky. Hip wiggle hip wiggle. Smiley smile.

Left the tarts' wardrobe.

Just as we were about to hit the dance floor Jas said, "What about knickers?"

I looked at her. "Yes, what about them?"

"Have you got any on?"

Is she truly mad? But then I couldn't actually remember putting them on. When did I put them on? I remember putting the skirt on and my bra and top, but knickers?

Which ones were they? Oh God. Perhaps I had forgotten and then I would fall over and reveal my front and back bottoms to the world.

Or Sven would pick me up like he very often did when he was doing his frenzied *Saturday Night Fever* routine.

I dashed back into the loos.

Knicker alert over. I blame Jas entirely – she is so obsessed with underwear.

9:00 p.m.

Vair vair dark in the club – and rammed. We edged around to the bar; it took a while to get used to the dark. Especially if your eyes were weighed down with one pound of mascara and talcum powder. Dave the Laugh was about an inch away from my nose before I saw him. "Hello, Kittykat, you're back."

I smiled at him and then Rachel popped her head over his shoulder. "Hi Georgie, cool to see you."

She is always so alarmingly pleased to see me. Why? There's nothing wrong with her, but I'm Dave's friend, not hers. She pulled on Dave's arm and said, "Come and dance, babe."

He looked at me and I for once had the upper whatsit. I said, "Yeah, babe, go dance."

He gave me a cross-eyed look and went off to dance.

Rollo and his mates were all there at the bar with Jools, Mabs and Ellen hanging on their every word. Pathetico. I would never do that. Everyone was there.

I said to Jas, "Jas, just nod your head up and down wisely. You don't have to talk. In fact, I'd rather you didn't. I want you to be my decoy duck while I look around for any sign of Masimo."

Jas tried to have a strop, but I stopped her by saying, "You know I am only asking you to do this because you are my vair vair bestest pallsie in the whole world. Also, if you help me with this I will let you sing Tom's song to me."

Jas perked up then. "Yip yip, he's back in five days. I only came out to help you with all your boy troubles, you know."

I was going to give her a friendly dead arm for being so annoying, when some bulky girl trod on my toe as she was going by with her lardy mates. I shouted out, "Bloody hell in a hand basket, ouch ouch! Bollocking bugger bugger bum!!!"

Jas said, "Are you sure your shoes are OK?"

I said, "Jas, some complete imbecile of gigantic proportions has just trodden on my foot. That is why I am leaping like a loon."

I might actually have to slip off for a quick lie down in the loos and put my feet up on the loo seat.

But then "all pain dropped away from my tootsies forsooth", as Billy so eloquently put it in his famous sonnet "Ode to my feet". Masimo came up to the bar.

He looked mega-cool (and a half). He doesn't look like English boys. He's more sophis. He was wearing a cool, pale blue Italian suit with a T-shirt. Like me, he was wearing fabby shoes. (Although his didn't have kitten heels and he didn't look like he was going to wet himself.)

I put my shoulders back to give a bit of nunga emphasis (looking round first to make sure I didn't knock anyone over). Also, I let my mouth drop open a bit and put my tongue behind my bottom teeth. Like Britney Spears but without the big tongue piercing.

I was deliberately not acknowledging Masimo. I was absolutely tip-top full of glaciosity.

Jas, Ellen, and Mabs were, however, full of stupidosity. They all came crowding round me going, "Have you seen him?

Have you seen him? He's at the bar, over there – look, can you see him?" And so on. Soooo annoying and uncool.

I was still doing my tongue behind the teeth thing, so I said, "Thlear off, tho away, thleave me ayown."

I pretended to wave at someone in Masimo's direction, and the Luuurve God caught my eye and smiled. I slightly smiled, and he began to come across to me. Oh I love him I love him. But no! Remember the plan. I smiled again and then I forced myself to walk away.

And not look back. Cor, how difficult was this? It was like walking with my feet facing in one direction and my body facing in the opposite direction trying to snog him. Like a really crap mime artist. But I must do it. I must keep up my glaciosity.

Also, I was trying to make a good impression from the back. I was concentrating so much on crap mime-walking, hip-wiggling, hair-flicking and eschewing the Luuurve God with a firm hand that I went nunga-nunga-first into Dave the Laugh. Again.

He said, "Settle down, lads," straight to my basoomas. Cheeky cat.

However, he was the Hornmeister and there was no sign

of Rachel, so I told him what I'd just done. I said, "You would have been proud. Masimo came over to me and I walked away with glaciosity at all times. What do you think tacticwise?"

He looked a bit funny. If I didn't know that he was a callous Hornmeister, I would have said he looked a bit sad, but I must have been wrong, because he said, "Excellent work. Keep it up. What handbag has he got tonight?"

Then Rachel came bounding up like a friendly red setter. Dave was nice to her, but he looked a bit cornered. If I were her I would give him a bit more space. Blimey, I am suddenly full of wisdomosity about relationships. I have become an expert in the oven of love.

9:30 p.m.

No sign of my rival in love, the incredibly useless stick insect of the universe and back. Good. Oh, maybe she's dead. How sad. Never mind.

The Stiff Dylans are coming on in a minute.

9:40 p.m.

Wow, the place has gone hog wild!!! Girls were shrieking

when Masimo came to the microphone and said "*Ciao*. We are back."

10:15 p.m.
I am quite literally in a dance inferno. Hit it, lads! The whole club is kicking. All the boys are fit and cool and Masimo is a brilliant singer and sooooo sexy on stage.

10:35 p.m.
Girls were even trying to get up on the stage to get to the Stiff Dylans! One got up and managed to kiss Masimo on the cheek before she was pulled away by a bouncer. Vair vair embarrassing. The final straw was when Nauseating P. Green tried to get up on stage. No danger of her managing that. She got one knee on and then just jumped up about a foot and came back down again. She would have been stuck there for eternity going up and down, but a bouncer came and pulled her away. Her new enormous glasses were on sideways.

Attractive.

10:40 p.m.
I'm sweating a bit so I had better go and cool myself down

in the loos; the last thing a Luuurve God wants is a slippery girlfriend. I have been doing some of my best moves in front of him. Just subtly, you know, nothing flash, although I did have to shove Jas quite hard once or twice to get her to let me in. Now and again I have glanced at him and then looked away. Wet Lindsay has been dancing in front of him with her eyes fixed on him like she was trying to hypnotise him.

I said to Ro Ro, "As the Swan of Avon said in his famous snogging comedy *Midsummer Night's Snog*, 'When you wanteth to snog a Luuurve God, do not prithee danceth about like a prat with stick-insect legs.'"

Rosie said, "Ye are wiseth in the extremeth, my palleth. Billy also saideth, 'Forsooth and lack a day, do not have ye a tiny forehead, otherwise you are simply asketh for a duffing-up scenario... eth.'"

Then we laughed like the proverbial draineth.

10:50 p.m.

As I went to the loos I saw Rollo and Jools snogging for England on the steps. And then in the corridor by the loos I found Mabs snogging someone – I couldn't tell who it was boywise as I didn't recognise the back of his head. As I went by, Mabs opened her eyes and winked at me. What was she on about? Then she pointed at her wristwatch, with the other hand she held up three fingers, then she did the thumbsies up. Still snogging. What in the name of arse? I went into the loos.

In the tarts' enclosure

Blimey! Good job I did a make-up check; I looked like a red-faced loon.

Then I got it! Mabs was saying that she had got up to number six on the snogging scale – a kiss lasting over three minutes without a break!

Yes! She'll be thrilled as a thrilled thing on a thrilling holiday.

Unless it was Spotty Norman.

They were all at it. Apart from me. It was so long since I'd snogged anyone, I couldn't even remember what it felt like to snog. Perhaps I had lost my technique. I tried a quick snog on the back of my arm, but it was very difficult to tell the difference between arm and lipsies.

I must take my shoes off for a moment. I went into a piddly-diddly kiosk and sat down on the loo seat. Hmmm, my feet looked a bit red and swollen; maybe I should take my shoes off. But if I got them off I might never get them back on.

Perhaps if I just lay down on the floor and put my feet above my head on the loo they would go down a bit.

I got down on the floor and put my feet up. Ohhh, that was a bit better. I heard a door open and Wet Lindsay said, "What's going on?"

This really weedy voice answered, "Well, it looks like they're going to be having a break any time."

It was Astonishingly Dim Monica, the missing link between human beings and frogs.

Wet Lindsay said, "OK, I'd better get in there."

ADM said, "Treat 'em mean, keep 'em keen!"

And Lindsay said, "I don't think I have any worries about keenness if Thursday is anything to go by. They are very passionate, the Italians."

And she laughed.

God I hate her.

I lay on the floor for a moment feeling really really bad and miz, but then I remembered that I was not a facsimile of a sham. I was following my dream, I was living the dream! I struggled up to my feet. Owwww... *Sacré* bloody *bleu*.

Back in the club

The band were having a break – no sign of them. I could see Wet Lindsay hovering around near the dressing-room door. Appalling tart. The Ace Gang were all off grooving.

Rosie shouted over, "Come and dance, we're having a groovathon."

I said, "I think I'll sit this one out and just, you know, absorb the vibes."

Rosie said, "You mean your feet are hurting because you are wearing baby's shoes."

I gave her my cross-eyed Klingon look and she nutcased off.

Sitting down, I was doing a bit of shoulder dancing to the music when an arm appeared in front of me and handed me a drink. It was a brown arm, it had a gold ring on the third finger. I looked up, and it was Masimo's arm. And he was attached to it.

He smiled down at me. "*Ciao*, you are having tired from dancing?"

I went red – thank God it was dark. I took a big gulp from the drink and practically choked myself, but I managed to say, "Yes, I mean, *sí*. I am indeed having a tired from dancing, yes indeedy."

He said, "It is long since I have seen you. I am glad you came. I would like, if you would like, to have your telephone number."

Oh now, what was the right response to that? Glaciosity requires that I say something like, "Maybe some other time." But he is a Luuurve God. He is bending over me, his gorgey lips are only inches away from mine.

Anyway, I was saved the trouble of doing anything because Dom came over. "Hi, Georgia, long time no dig. How are you?"

Before I could say anything he went on to Masimo. "Listen, mate, sorry to drag you away, but some bloke wants to talk to us about a tour in the North. Can you come over?"

Masimo looked at me with those amazing amber eyes. "I will see you later."

And he touched my shoulder and squeezed it very gently.

Oh no, he had said it. He had said the famous "See you later".

Donner and bloody Blitzen. Absobloodylutely typico.

I have got such bad snog withdrawal!!!

Merde and merdy *merde merde merde*. And a half.

I hobbled over to the groovathon and bobbed around trying to talk to Rosie as Sven flung her about like a deflated balloon.

Pant pant, groove groove.

"He's asked me for my phone number!"

Rosie yelled, "Result! Or Resultio, as we must say!"

I looked across and I could see the Stiff Dylans talking to some bloke at a table. Masimo leaned back in his chair and balanced on one leg. The chair leg, I mean, you fools!! Not his leg. He looked across at me and just looked and locked eyes with me. He was doing sticky eyes with me. It was a moment of incredibilosity. However, it began to feel like a staring competition because the mascara on my eyes was vair heavy. Eventually he looked away because someone handed him a drink, so I could blink.

11:30 p.m.
Band back on.

I am sooo excited. I said to Jas, "Do you think I should accidentally hang around as he comes off stage at the next break?"

Jas looked like she was thinking, *Oh dear.*

I can't rely on her opinion. I must consult with the gang. I rounded them up eventually for a gang meeting in the tarts' wardrobe. I was going to ask the Hornmeister but he was slow dancing with Rachel and she had her head on his shoulder. He was stroking her hair, but as I passed he looked, I don't know, not like Dave the Laugh. So I thought I wouldn't ask about Masimo.

When Mabs emerged from her snogathon it turned out to be one of the trainee tossers she was snogging. I said, "Mabs, you have vair little pridenosity, that is one of Tosser Thompson's mates."

Mabs was a bit surly and covered in her own lippy. She looked like she had been attacked by a ferret. She said, "Well, I'm only practising on him."

Fair enough.

It was a moment or two before I realised that Sven was in the loos with us.

Rosie managed to persuade him to wait outside. I don't like to think what she promised him as a reward, but she did mention herrings...

I said, "Masimo wanted my phone number and I was

♡ 217

just about to give it to him."

Rosie said, "Oo-er, missus."

But I just looked at her and went on. "I was just about to give him my number, when Dom called him away. So now the thing is, should I hang around at the end of the set and give it to him?"

Rosie was just about to say oo-er again until I kicked her.

Ellen said, "Well, if, you know... if he asked you, and well, he asked you... that means, doesn't it, that he, you know... wants it."

We all looked at Ellen.

I said, "Anyway, what do you think I should do?"

Jas said, "I would hang around. I mean, it's ridiculous playing silly games, isn't it?"

Rosie said, "Yes, I think cut to the action – go up and give him the phone number and then leave."

Hmmmm. Yes, that sounded good. Everyone else was nodding. And when all of the Ace Gang nod, you know that... er... you know that a nod is as good as a wink to a blind badger.

We did the Klingon salute and make-up duties and then went out of the loos together. The others careered back on to the dance floor, apart from Mabs, because the trainee tosser was hanging around outside the door. I lurked at the back of the club near the tarts' wardrobes for a moment to sit down on the stairs. My tootsies were soooooo sore. I tried to ease my feet in my shoes but they wouldn't move. I must save my tootsies for a last walk across to give Masimo my telephone number.

12:30 a.m.
Outside the cloakroom getting our coats out. The band must be going to come out soon. I put my coat on slowly.

Dave the Laugh was with Rachel and she was linking up with him. He said, "S'later, Georgia."

And Rachel gave me a big hug goodbye. "Great to see you, Gee."

After they had gone I said to Jas, "Is it? Why? Why is she hugging me? We don't do hugging, do we? And we are very nearly mates."

Jas said, "I think it's nice that she's so friendly."

I didn't. It was weird. I went on. "Is she on the turn? Or perhaps there's a touch of the Froggy in her family? I must warn Dave."

I was so distracted by Rachel that at first I didn't sense the Luuurve presence. He was just coming out of the dressing room, putting his jacket on. How come even putting his jacket on was sexy?

I had the Particular and Cosmic Horn and a heavy dose of red-bottomosity.

He turned round to say something to one of the others, and Wet Lindsay appeared like the Bride of Dracula. She just appeared from nowhere. She was playing with her hair and she trailed her hand across Masimo's arm. He looked round and saw her and smiled. She kissed his cheek and said something in his ear. He said something back and then she whispered something else. He looked at her and sort of shrugged his shoulders. She smiled and then linked arms with him and they went off together.

Oh God.

1:00 a.m.
And we had to walk all the way home because we had done the usual "Jas's dad is picking us up" to my dad and "Georgia's dad is picking us up" to Jas's. In a fit of

desperation I thought about phoning Vati and telling him we were stuck, but then I would have to talk to him, and I didn't want to talk ever again.

1:30 a.m.
I managed to sneak in. Actually, I didn't really need to sneak because Dad was snoring so loudly in his bedroom. And Gordy was snoring in the lavatory. And, oh good, Libby was snoring in my bed.

Lying quite literally in my bed of pain
2:30 a.m.
I have tried to get my shoes off but I am so tired and upset I can't be bothered to struggle with them. So I've left them on and put my jimmyjams on over them. My feet hurt like billio, but not as much as my heart.

2:35 a.m.
What is it with boys and Wet Lindsay?

I dither about for hours thinking, *Shall I have glaciosity or shall I have boldnosity? What botty huggers shall I wear? Is the orang-utan gene making a surprise appearance?* and so on, for hours and hours. And she just goes up to him and says, "Come with me," and off he goes.

Unbelievable.

2:40 a.m.

I am not going to give up this time, though, I have had my heart burned in the oven too many times.

I am going to think of a cunning plan.

2:45 a.m.

Oh brilliant, Angus and Gordy are playing the mouse game with my shoefeet.

Owwwwwwwww.

2:46 a.m.

Libby woke up from her snoring extravaganza and sat up with her arms crossed. She said, "Bad Georgia. Sshhhhhhh!"

I tried to cuddle her but she got the hump and stomped off with Gordy under one arm to go to her own bed.

Rejected by my sister as well.

And she didn't even leave Sandra behind.

Sunday June 5th

10:00 a.m.

I woke up and I saw my shoefeet looking at me from the bottom of the bed.

Then I felt the pain... but I am going to have to bear it and take them off.

10:15 a.m.

Oh please. My shoes are embedded in my feet. My skin has been cut by the straps and then in the night everything has all swollen up. You can't even see the straps because the flesh has covered them up. Oh brilliant. Now I will have to have my feet cut off.

10:30 a.m.

Worse than that, I am going to have to ask Mum for help because I can't walk. I will never never laugh at Slim's feet again, because I have got them.

11:00 a.m.

Mum bustled into my room. When I heard her I put my shoefeet under the blankets. She said, "Come on and have

♥ 223

some breakfast. Dad's taken Libbs round to Josh's, so it's just you and me. We can do something nice if you like."

I said, "It will have to be something that doesn't involve walking about."

She said, "Don't tell me you are tired. Honestly, I had so much energy at your age – I'd go to parties and then play tennis the next day."

I said, "Well, I would like to play tennis, believe me, but Parky Elvis would never let me play in high heels – it would ruin his courts."

Mum said, "What are you talking about?"

I had to tell her about the shoes. Then I showed her my feet. She went ballisticisimus. "You STUPID stupid girl. Honestly, you have done some stupid stupid things in your time, but this takes the biscuit of stupidity. How could you do this to yourself? I told you about those shoes! Look at your lovely feet – ruined!!!"

And so on for about four centuries.

Mum had a go at getting them off herself, but I couldn't bear the pain, and in the end she said, "I'm going to have to phone for the doctor. On a Sunday."

Oh nooooo. I am so humiliated.

Midday

I heard Mum phoning the doctor. She said, "I am so sorry to disturb you, doctor, but it's Georgia..."

There was a pause.

"No, no the elbows are, you know, quite stable, it's... well, she has got her shoes embedded in her feet."

1:00 p.m.

I saw Dr Clooney's car arrive in the driveway and he got out. I hobbled back into bed – ouch ouch and double ouch.

Thank goodness Vati was out.

I heard giggling from downstairs.

1:25 p.m.

Oh yes, that's right, Mutti, just chat and flirt with Dr Clooney while I lie up here with my dancing days over.

Honestly.

Eventually Mum and Dr Clooney came up. My mum had changed into her short black dress and done her hair and make-up. Vair vair sad.

Dr Clooney gave me his crinkly smile. "Well, well, this is a first for me."

He is nice, though, very reassuring and funny. He didn't ramble on at me. He just looked at my feet and pulled a bit and I went "Owwwwww."

Then he said, "Hmmm, I'm going to have to give you a local anaesthetic and cut them off."

And I said, "Oh, doctor, can't you save them?"

And he started saying that he meant the shoes, not my feet, and I said, "I know. Can't you save them?"

Mum gave me her worst look, but Dr Clooney thought it was vair *amusant*.

2:00 p.m.

This is quite nice, actually, in a painful way. Dr Clooney cut off the straps and pulled the bits out with tweezers. He even had to put some stitches in the deep cuts in my feet. It hurt A LOT but I was brave as a bee on army manoeuvres. They are all bandaged up. Mum is bringing me snacks.

She sat down on my bed and I let her, I don't know why, I am probably weak.

She said, "So, Stumpy, did you have a nice time last night at least?"

I blurted out, "Well, it was megafab at first because Masimo asked me for my phone number, but then at the end Wet Lindsay made him go home with her."

Mum said, "I used to know a girl like Wet Lindsay. She got married to a boy I really liked."

I said, "Oh thanks, Mum, you're really cheering me up."

And she said, "Well, every cloud has a silver lining, because she is really really unhappily married. So all's well that ends well."

Sometimes my mum, and I don't want to get carried away by this, but sometimes she can be almost like a real person.

4:00 p.m.

It's quite cosy just me and Mum together. I was asking her stuff about how to make any twit fall in love with you (without actually mentioning that I had read her book, otherwise she would know that I had been rifling through her drawers and unreasonably lose her rag).

As we slurped our fifth hot choccy, Mum had a quick touch of wisdomosity. She said, "I think you should just relax and be yourself. What is the point of being a callous sophisticate, or tricking a boy into liking you? He's bound to find out eventually. It's the only real advice I can give you. Be your own natural self."

I said, "Like when you put that black dress on and loads of make-up when Dr Clooney came round?"

She stood up. "Well, be yourself within reason. At least get the right size shoes next time."

We have decided not to bother Vati with the shoefoot incident and settled for "girl trouble" until Wednesday, when I should be able to walk again.

I said, "You mean I get time off from Stalag 14 for good behaviour? Oh, thank you, thank you, Mutti, you know how much I love you."

I have agreed to be very nice to Vati and Libby and Mutti for the next couple of days in recognition of Mum's act of charity.

Midnight
I wonder what Masimo did when they left the gig?

I wonder what number they got up to?

Erlack. Shutup, mind, shutup.

Monday June 6th

8:30 a.m.

Well, I may get pretend-ill a lot. Dad brought me a cup of tea, and Mum phoned Jas and told her I'd be off school with a tummy bug for a couple of days.

Mmmm snuggle snuggle.

Ouch ouchy ouch.

10:00 a.m.

This is the life (ish). I am lolling in bed and everyone is out. I think I'll just hobble downstairs for a snack.

10:30 a.m.

I haven't been in the house on my own on a weekday for ages. It is an unknown world of peace and quiet and... cats. So this is what happens when we, the baldy folk, are out – the house turns into Kittykat Heaven.

Naomi is stretched out comfortably on the front-room sofa. I hope she has enough cushions. She sleepily opened one eye when I put my head round the door, but seeing I had no snacks she went back to sleep. Make yourself at home, Ms Minx.

Gordy is snoozing on the telephone table, probably

expecting an urgent call. And Angus seems to be covered in jam and lolling about on Mum's silk blouse that she left on the ironing board. She will go ballisticisimus.

I would move them, but I can't be expected to because of my condition.

10:40 a.m.
I opened the fridge for snacksies and took out the butter. It has a small paw mark in it. Surely the furry maniacs haven't learned how to open the fridge door? Freaky-deaky. They'll be dressing up in our clothes soon and driving the clown car off for a cat picnic.

Good.

12:00 p.m.
Fed up now. I wonder what the Ace Gang are doing? I bet they're talking about the gig. I bet they're talking about me and Masimo. They had better not say anything bad.

What is there to say that is bad?

I hope they're keeping up the staring campaign against Wet Lindsay. I'm glad I am not in today because she can't show off in front of me.

2:00 p.m.

I have shared two boyfriends with her.

2:10 p.m.

But Robbie, er, I mean the Guitar Plucker only went out with her because she was so upset when he tried to dump her. And she said she was engaged to him when she wasn't. I think she must be a bit unhinged.

She should be.

Actually, the Guitar Plucker acted very nicely about her and me. What I mean is, he dumped her. If anyone is asking for a good dumping, it's her. If he hadn't gone to Kiwi-a-gogo land, all of this wouldn't have happened.

I wonder what would have happened.

3:00 p.m.

I got out his letter and photo, which I had hidden at the back of my drawer. I took them back into bed. What does he say?

"I think about you a lot."

Huh.

He didn't think about me enough to not go to the other side of the world.

He was my first proper love. They say you never forget that.

I looked at the photo. He was vair good-looking, and he was very nice to me.

Even in front of his mates he would always put his arm round me and didn't try to hide me away.

3:45 p.m.
I thought about all the good times.

Maybe I should write to him?

4:00 p.m.
I think I will write.

And maybe send a photo.

I could send him one of when we were in Hamburger-a-gogo. It would remind him of the plans we had to go there with the band.

Ha.

I won't send him the one of me riding the bucking-bronco stool.

4:10 p.m.

Nor the one with that very very old bloke in the Elvis outfit.

4:25 p.m.

Or me at Davy Crockett's diner in the furry beaver hat.

5:00 p.m.

Or one of the ones me and Jas took in private with the bison horns.

No one must ever see those. No one. Not another living soul.

I must remind Jas.

I'll do it now.

5:15 p.m.

Phoned Jas.

"Jas, it's me."

"Hellooooo, how are your feet?"

"Bandaged up. Listen, you must never show anyone our bison-horn pictures."

"Oh, blimey. Hahahahaha. I'd forgotten about them. What a hoot and a half that was."

"Yes, I know that we thought it was very *amusant* at the time, Jas, but pictures of us in the nuddy-pants wearing just bison horns might, well you know, if they fell into the wrong hands."

She was chewing and thinking.

"Oh yeah, I see what you mean. Well, yes, I will only show them to Tom when he gets back. Do you know how many minutes it is until he's back? It's two hundred thousand—"

"Jas, shut up about minutes – you are not a Time Lord, more's the pity. Tell me everything that happened at Stalag 14 today."

6:00 p.m.

Well, that was a very interesting conversation. Not. I will tell you what happened at Stalag 14. Nothing.

I said to Jas, "Were people worried about me, that I had this tummy bug and so on?"

She said, "No, because we all knew it was because your shoes were too small. We said they were too small for your huge feet."

"Jas, I haven't got huge feet."

"You have now! Hahahahahaha!"

Oh charming. I said, "Oh yes, very funny, Jas. If you want a really good laugh why don't you just pop down to casualty."

6:35 p.m.
Anyway, the short and short of it is that no one said anything interesting, and even Wet Lindsay wasn't there because she was doing home study.

6:45 p.m.
Ohmygod. I've just had a horrible thought. Home study – that could mean home study with Masimo.

Surely he can't like her that much.

Surely.

Tuesday June 7th

I'm sick of being an invalid now.

I am sooooo bored and I am, it has to be said, completely hairless – I have spent hours plucking.

6:30 p.m.
Phoned Jas.

She isn't home. They have all gone off to the pictures.

Boo.

I'm even looking forward to my family coming home – that should give you some idea of how desperate I am.

6:50 p.m.

Mum and Dad and Libbs came in.

"Gingee, Gingee, it's meeeeeeeeeeee!!!"

I could hear her panting up the stairs to my room. She kicked open my bedroom door and ran from the door and leaped on to the bed, covering me with kisses.

"I LOBE you, my big big sister."

I couldn't get her off me. "Libby, just let me—"

"Kissy kissy kiss, snoggy snog."

"That's enough, now let me—"

"Mmmmmm, groovy baby."

What is she talking about? She is supposed to be going to nursery school to learn how to grow up, not turn into an even madder person.

Then she stood up on the bed and started thrusting her hips out and singing her favourite: "Sex bum, sex bum, I'm a sex bum."

Quite spectacularly mad.

7:30 p.m.

Mmmmm, quite nice supper of shepherd's pie. On a tray in bed. Mum didn't make it herself, of course, but at least she bothered to buy it. I think it may have given me the strength to go downstairs and watch TV to try and forget my sorrows.

7:33 p.m.

Oh no, I can't, otherwise Dad will spot the shopping bags I have on the end of my feet.

Maybe I can ask him to bring the TV up to my room. It's the least you can do when there's a sick person in the house.

7:35 p.m.

Just about to suggest this when I heard the roar of an engine.

Knowing my life, it would be Grandad on a motorbike in a leather all-in-one suit. And Maisie on the back in a knitted bikini.

I peeped out of my window – and practically fell out of it.

It was Masimo!!! Honestly. On his scooter. He was under my window and just switching the engine off.

I must run run like the wind to... oh no, I couldn't run. I must hobble, hobble like the wind to... no, no, what I must do is – I must remain calm. Calm calm. While all around you everyone is losing their minds you must, you must... put some bloody make-up on immediately, you complete arse!!

7:38 p.m.
Scrabble, scrabble, mascara... lippy and gloss... eyeshadow... please please don't do shaky hand now – I don't want to be a panda with huge feet!!!

Fluffy hair fluffy hair...

What was going on now? What? What???

Mid mascara, did a hobble-trot to the window and looked out.

There was just his scooter there. Like the Vespa Celeste. Had Angus eaten him?

Then I heard the doorbell ring.

Ohgoddygod.

Put something on. Disguise the feet!

Easier said than done.

I must have something.

Scrabbled through my wardrobe.

What about my extra-long jeans? Yes, yes, good thinking. Extra-long jeans, bit of a crouchy leg and... I looked in the full-length mirror. Yes, yes, that would do, you couldn't see my feet at all. I must remember to crouch though, and not hobble.

Right, right, I am ready for when Dad starts his ludicrous shouting up the stairs. It's OK though, because he will just say tummy bug, not shoes cut off.

I must not mention shoes cut off. No one should.

Good, good, that is good.

Excellent.

7:40 p.m.
What was going on?

Couldn't they understand what Masimo was saying? His English wasn't that bad.

8:00 p.m.
What *was* going on? Surely Masimo hadn't come round to see my mum and dad, had he? With my life, I wouldn't be surprised by anything. Perhaps like Dave the Laugh, Masimo fancies my mum.

♡ 239

I crept and shuffled to the top of the stairs. They were in the living room, so I could just hear the muffled sound of voices. Then Libby came bustling along the hall and opened the door to the front room. She waddled into the lounge, saying, "Gordy has done a big poo in his din dins."

Dear Lord.

8:10 p.m.

I had to rush back into my bedroom because Mum suddenly came out of the room to the kitchen and shouted up to me, "Georgia, I know you're at the top of the stairs. Come down – you have a visitor and your father wants to speak to you."

My father?

Wants to speak to me?

I have a visitor?

It's like *Blithering Heights*. If Masimo is dressed in tight breeches and a cravat, I will truly go mad.

I felt really really sick.

I went into the kitchen first.

Mum was making filter coffee. Blimey. I said to her, "What is going on?"

She said, "Oh, we were just having a chat with Masimo. He's lovely, isn't he?"

"Having a chat? Having a CHAT? You have left Vati having a CHAT with someone I never ever want him to talk to about anything. Having a chat about what?"

"Well, he has come to ask us, and in particular your father, if it's all right for him to take you out to dinner next week."

I was quite literally speechless.

8:15 p.m.
Mum made me go into the front room.

Masimo was sitting on the sofa with Libby on his knee. He stood up with her in his arms when I walked in and then he smiled. And when he did that my heart sang. Despite the fresh hell that was about to occur, he was sooooooo gorgey.

Vati was standing up in front of the fireplace with his hands behind his back. Then I realised he was smoking a cigar. He never smoked cigars except at Christmas, and then he was sick. What the hell was going on?

He said, "Ah, hello, Georgia. Masimo and I have just been having a chat."

Oh dear God he was using that word again.

Masimo said, "*Ciao*, Georgia."

My vati said, "Do sit down, Georgia. Connie."

It was like being in a cross between a horror film and *My Fair Lady*.

I didn't know what else to do, so I sat down and so did Mum. As soon as we did, Vati and Masimo sat down as well. I fought an overwhelming desire to stand up again to see if they would stand up too.

Dad said, "Masimo has come round to ask if it is all right for him to take you out, and I think after careful thought and a few ground rules that... it would be... acceptable to your mother and myself."

Has he really snapped? He works for the Waterboard, drowning people and driving them out of their homes, but he is not in the Mafia.

He went rambling on about curfews and behaviour. Like the Godfather. He will probably expect us to call him Il Ministrone. Complete and utter bollocks about honour and his family reputation and so on. I was so so embarrassed. And Masimo just said stuff like, "Of course, I will, how you say, take *molto – mi dispiace*, I am sorry for my English, I will

242

take great care of your daughter."

He smiled at me. "She will even have her own helmet."

And Mum laughed like a crazy person, like "helmet" was the funniest word she had ever heard.

9:00 p.m.

I only got a chance to speak to Masimo right at the end of the nightmare scenario. When he went out to go off on his bike I went out to the gate with him. I said, "Masimo, I am so sorry about my parents. I am dispiaggio times a million about them."

He smiled and said, "I thought it was the only way I will get your attention. Now I have your attention, no?"

"Oh yes, you have sure as sure as… eggs… have my attention, matey."

He laughed.

"I like it when you speak, it is like…"

"Rubbish?"

He laughed again and handed me a piece of paper.

"Here, this is for you. Phone me, *cara*, and let me know if you still would like to see me on Tuesday. *Ciao*."

He looked at me with that unwavering look he has. Oh

dear God, I had crumbly knees and jelloid knickers and I sooo wanted to go to the piddly-diddly department.

Then he roared off.

9:05 p.m.
Went back into the house. With a bit of luck I could get in without being seen by the seeing-eye dogs. But oh no, no such luck. Vati came out of the front room.

"He seems like a nice young chap. Keen on sports and so on. Good family, healthy lifestyle."

I said, "Shiny nose, glossy coat, that sort of thing."

He said, "I said to your mum that you're not old enough for boys, you should be concentrating on your studies."

Oh, blimey, I had wandered into the twilight world of Daddom. I wandered off as quickly as I could hobble, saying, "Oooh, do you know, Dad, I've come over all queasy. I must go back to bed."

In my bedroom
Yesssssss! Double yesss and wow! I had a date with the Luuurve God. I looked at the piece of paper he had given me. It said, "Masimo 766739. Phone me. Please."

244

I had his phone number. No waiting around for him to call me. No more s'later for me! I am a s'later-free zone!

10:00 p.m.

God, I'm happy.

The photo of the Guitar Plucker was on the bed looking at me.

Maybe I will write to him.

As a friend.

A loving old friend.

A loving friend who has gone on to more Italian-Stallion-type things!

I wish I could ring everyone and tell them. I am deffo going to school tomorrow, even if Jas has to carry me there.

10:30 p.m.

I will never sleep with excitemondo!

What shall I wear? Are we really going to go out to dinner or is that just a snogging ploy?

I've never been out to dinner with a boy before.

11:00 p.m.

I tell you this, I am not having cappuccino and the foam-beard experience. If we are going to dinner I'd better plan what I'm having in advance because I don't want the attractive dribbly tomato sauce effect on my snogging arena (mouth).

"What PANTS through yonder window breaks?"

Wednesday June 8th
Stalag 14
Feet miraculously better. I am down to light bandages now!!

But even if I had no feet, I would be walking on air... Hahahahahaha, that's quite a good joke.

I said that to Jas, "It's a good joke, isn't it, Jazzy Spazzy?"

She said, "What is?"

In the corridor
9:00 a.m.
Saw Wet Lindsay, hahahaha. She glared at me and told me to hurry up to class. Hurry up yourself, old dumpee thong.

Fives court emergency tactical meeting

Rosie said, "'Be prepared' is always my motto."

Ellen said, "I didn't know you were a Girl Guide."

Rosie said, "Didn't you? Oh yes, me and Sven are keen Girl Guides, dib dib dib and so forth."

The whole thing would have disintegrated into madnosity, so I quickly said, "So what do you think I should do? How shall I handle it? Do you think he is really going to take me out to dinner?"

After much consultation and nodding, the gang have decided that we should have a mock date to prepare me for my date.

We are all going to meet round Ro Ro's place on Saturday when her parents are at the cricket. We're going to practise for my hot date. There will be snacks. But no Sven.

I had to beg and plead with Rosie. She said, "He would be vair vair useful, he could give us the boy point of view."

I said, "Couldn't he give you the boy point of view and then you pass it on to me, or you will just snog all day in front of us. Also, he is bound to smash something to smithereens."

Rosie has reluctantly agreed to ban him.

At home

6:00 p.m.

I am dying to tell Dave the Laugh.

Phoned him when the olds went out to a parents evening for Libby at the local school. Surely no school is going to take her on. She has been forbidden to sing the "Bum arse song" and not allowed to take Gordy. I still think it was a mistake to let her wear her leopard outfit, because a) it is for a child half her size and b) she becomes a leopard in it. But you can't tell people.

Anyway, where was I? Oh yes, Dave the Laugh.

I called him. I hoped my best friend Rachel was not there.

Dave answered. "Hello, Sensation Seeker."

"Dave, it's me. Something vair vair great and *bon* has happened. I am going on a date with Masimo. He came round on his scooter and asked my dad if he could take me to dinner. He asked my dad if he could take me to dinner!!!"

Dave said, "What an amazing bunch of crawlers the Italians are."

"Dave!!! Don't you get it? He has asked me out! I am going out with him!"

Dave said, "Well, I'm glad for you, Sex Kitty, but

♡ 249

remember what I said; he may be playing the field. He may just be blowing his Cosmic Horn."

He sounded a bit funny.

"You sound a bit funny, Dave. Are you all right?"

Dave said, "Well, not really, I had to finish with Rachel."

Finish with Rachel? I said, "Why? I mean, she's so... Well, she is so, you know... isn't she?"

Blimey, I've turned into Ellen.

Dave said, "It just wasn't right. But anyway, she's very upset. She's just gone actually. She came round and cried and I feel pretty bad."

I said, "Oh, I'm sorry."

But actually I'm not sorry at all. After I'd rung off I told Jas that, because she was my next phone call. It's not often I get a telephone window of opportunity in my house, so I am packing all my calls in.

Jas said, "Why are you bothered who Dave goes out with? He is not in your harem or anything. And another thing: Rachel was nice – not like you."

God, she can be annoying. I wish I hadn't called her now, especially as she did that "Guess how many minutes it is until Tom gets home?" thing again.

Saturday June 11th

2:00 p.m.

All the gang gathered at Rosie's for my practice date.

Rosie said she would be Masimo, and the rest of them would watch and be the judges, like in a sort of snogging *Come Dancing*.

Come Snogging, in fact.

2:10 p.m.

Rosie went off to her bedroom. She said, "I'm going to be Masimo, so I have to get in the mood for luuurve."

She came back five minutes later wearing a false beard, with a banana down her jeans.

I said, "Why have you got a banana down your jeans?"

Rosie said, "It was Sven's suggestion. He said it is representative of the pant python."

Ellen said, "I, er... do you mean like a boy's, er, well..."

Rosie said, "Exactomondo, my little pally." Which was a bit off-putting, actually.

Jas said, "OK, let's get on, because I have to get home earlyish. It's only ninety-nine hours till Tom gets home and I must prepare myself. What will you do when you first see him?" She pointed to Rosie, who was walking in a very peculiar way and waggling her beard. "There he is – tall, tanned Italian, sophisticated. So what do you do?"

I said, "Er, leap on him and snog him within an inch of his life? Taking care not to strangle myself on his false beard, or disturb his banana."

Jools said, "What does it say in the *How to Make Any Twit Fall in Love with You* book?"

Mabs was officially in charge of the book, so she looked up "first impressions".

3:00 p.m.

I have to hip wiggle up to him, look at him, look away, fiddle with my hair and do a bit of flicking. If I have any spare time I need to lick my lips a bit.

Mabs said, "The book says you should say something light and interesting to start the conversation. Also, if he says anything funny, you have to laugh like the proverbial drain."

I did hip wiggle, flicky, licky over to Rosie, while the rest of them sat looking and chewing. Rosie said (in what she imagines is an Italian accent but actually sounds like a fool), "*Ciao.*"

I said, "*Ciao*. Er, *prego*."

"*Ciao*."

All the gang were ogling me.

I said, "Masimo, did you know that the Spartans... you know in the old days of Sparta, which is quite nearish to Italy..."

Rosie had pretended to fall asleep. She said, "Get on with it."

I said, "Well, they used to keep teenage boys half-starved so that they had to go out and steal food, and if they got caught they would beat them to within an inch of their lives."

They all just looked at me.

Mabs said, "Do you call that light and interesting?"

I do actually. That is the deep sadnosity of my life; I find it vair difficult to be as superficial as others.

Jools said, "Think of something that he's interested in – think of something to do with Rome or something."

I tried again. "Did you know that the Pope has people who watch him poo to make sure he is a bloke and not a woman, because of Pope Joan?"

Rosie said, "You are not, as such, getting the hang of this, are you?"

An hour later

I am allowed to mention music, the weather, or something to do with him.

I said, "Yeah, but all I know about him is that I fancy the arse off him."

5:00 p.m.

After four packets of reviving Pringles we have managed to decide on, "*Ciao*, great to see you." and "What a fine evening."

Providing it is not tipping it down, which would make me a fool.

Now on to the meal.

Essentially, I have to pretend to eat a lot, but not really eat anything in case I choke to death.

Jas said, "You could have a nourishing soup, but don't do that slurping thing that you do."

I said, "What slurping thing?"

Jas said, "Oh, I can't go in to it now, I have to be off. I'm just saying don't do it."

And she went off.

How annoying is she?

6:00 p.m.

I have to listen to him a LOT.

Jools said, "And when you laugh, don't do your ad hoc laughing and let your nose spread all over your face."

6:30 p.m.

Then we got on to the snogging bit.

I said, "Do you think Italians snog the same as English boys?"

Rosie said, "I don't know if they do anything different with their tongues or what their ear work is like. You will have to give us a complete and full report. What number will you let him go up to on the first date?"

"I thought number six. A kiss lasting over three minutes without a break suggests deep sensuality without going that little bit too far into acting like a tart."

Then Rosie said, "Finally, as you haven't had any snogging practice for a while, try an experimental snog on the back of my leg."

What???

Absolutely not, not a snowball's chance in hell.

No and three times NO.

6:45 p.m.

On my knees snogging the back of Rosie's leg while the Ace Gang watch me.

Why am I doing this?

Rosie was shouting instructions. "Yes, yes, that's good. Good. And breathe. Too much teeth!! Too much teeth!!! A bit more sucky. Flicky tongue and... finish."

Good grief.

Have you ever snogged the back of someone's leg? Someone who is one of your mates and is wearing a false beard? Well, I hope you never have to, that is all I'm saying.

7:00 p.m.

I said as I was leaving, "Do you think I should ask him what his intentions are *vis à vis* Old Thongy?"

Mabs said, "I think you should act as if she doesn't exist and just find a way to subtly undermine her."

Hmmm. Good advice.

We are indeedy the Wise Women of the Forest of Snog.

Monday June 13th
English
2:00 p.m.

I have never laughed so much in my entire life. Today we had our first full rehearsal of *MacUseless*.

And what is even more vair vair amusing is that the Foxwood boys came to the rehearsal and Dave the Laugh was one of them.

The whole production is bound for the history books of life.

Dave and the lads were bussed in to the school and it was absolute pandemonium. Every girl in the school got up from their desk and started waving and screeching out the windows as the lads trooped across the playground. Hawkeye and her special storm troopers threatened us with embalming, beheading, etc., but no one paid any attention.

Those of us in the play went down to the main hall for our usual tongue-lashing from the enormous bee woman (Slim). The boys were all together at the back when we came in. As I passed by, Hawkeye said, "Georgia Nicolson, are you wearing mascara?"

I said, "It's for the bright lights, Miss Heaton. If you don't

♥ 257

wear eye make-up the audience can't see the expression, and that actually detracts from the emotional impact of—"

She said, "Shut up."

Then she picked on Ellen. "Ellen, why are you wearing lip gloss?"

"It's for the play, Miss Heaton."

"Oh, yes, and what part are you playing?"

When Ellen said she was a witch, she was made to go to the loos and take off her lip gloss.

When Slim took to the stage, the lads started softly singing, "Who ate all the pies, who ate all the pies?"

Slim was shaking like a loon on shaking tablets.

"That's enough. Quieten down. I expect grown-up behaviour from all of you. You are being given the opportunity to show us that our trust in you is not misplaced. I know that I can rely on you all to act with decorum and maturity."

And that's when the first stink bomb went off.

Backstage

Mr Attwood, our part-time caretaker and full-time loon, is having a spaz attack to end all spaz attacks. He was up near the roof fixing some lights to the lighting bar, and one of the lads removed his ladder.

Dave seems to have cheered up, even though he has broken Rachel's heart – allegedly. I said kindly, "She'll get over it."

Dave said, "As I have said many many times, Georgia, you are all heart. Are you going to be wearing a skimpy skirt and tights for your part as Macduff?"

And I said, "Why, was Macduff a transvestite?"

And Dave said, "Yes."

He is on "lights", which essentially means he hangs about backstage flirting and causing mayhem, and then switches a light on at the beginning. And he even did that at the wrong time.

Hanging around backstage with the lads and Dave the Laugh
3:15 p.m.

I have laughed so much that I almost forgot about Masimo. I told Dave about the fact that the Hamburgese, bless them, call knickers "panties", and it has entranced Dave beyond measure. He doesn't seem as heartbroken as he should be considering he has callously dumped his girlfriend.

♥ 259

3:20 p.m.

Dave has started this "pants" business, which he won't stop, and has given me an awful stitch. I cannot stop laughing. Miss Wilson is clearly going to kill me soon, but I can't stop. Essentially, he substitutes "pants" for everything, and it is vair vair *amusant* indeed. For instance, when everyone was on stage doing the battle scene, he started singing "Onward Christian Soldiers", but he introduced "pants" as a subtheme. So the lyrics in his Pants land are, "Onward Christian soldiers, marching as to war, with the PANTS of Jesus going on before." Although, as I pointed out, the American version would be "with the PANTIES of Jesus going on before."

3:30 p.m.

"The hills are alive with the sound of PANTS."

3:33 p.m.

Nauseating P. Green is doubling up her roles. She is my wife and also in charge of munitions.

260

3:35 p.m.

Well, when I say in charge of munitions, she has got a starting pistol thing that's going to be used for sound effects for the battle scenes. Also she has some bangers that she'll be letting off backstage with Spotty Norman as her co-idiot.

Miss Wilson told us that the first production of a Shakespants play in 1613 ended when a cannon used in the production set the thatched roof on fire and the theatre burned to the ground. So we can always hope for the best.

3:37 p.m.

Mr Attwood has got his fire buckets at the ready, so there is every chance of a conflagration. It would be a fitting end to his school career to be present when it burned down.

3:50 p.m.

Does anyone remember the world-renowned orange-juggling scene in *MacUseless*? No? Well, there is one in our production. Miss Wilson says it adds colour to the play. Hmmmm. How mad is she? It's during the banquet scene when MacUseless is planning to kill the other MacScottish person. She has got Melanie Griffiths and Mabs (who are trees in the later scene) to do the juggling.

They are vair vair useless at it but she has promised them they can wear false moustaches.

I said to Dave, "I am worried about Melanies nungas, I hope there is no unfortunate mix-up in the juggling bits."

You should see Spotty Norman and the other youth hanging around every time she's on stage, pretending to coil up electric cable and so on just so they can ogle her nungas.

Even Dave was watching her as oranges flew everywhere. He said, "That girl certainly has got a couple of areas of outstanding natural beauty. I hope they are adequately protected."

4:30 p.m.

As we left school Dave the Laugh walked along with us. He had his arm round me. It felt really, erm, friendly. Although, as it was Dave, his hand did sort of casually drift on to my nunga. I had to give him a yellow card and a stern warning. It obviously affected him because as he went off to his house he gave me a kiss on the mouth (!) and said, "S'later."

Hmmmmmm.

Home

Mum and Vati and Libbs and the furry freaks, have gone out on a clown-car expedition. Excellent.

Time to phone Masimo.

Put on my lippy gloss and a bit of mascara.

Right, here goes.

Better change out of my school uniform and put something gorgey but casual on.

Right, here goes.

Are boy entrancers going a bit far?

Right, here goes.

One minute later

"Jas."

"What?"

"I'm going to phone Masimo ."

"Good. Goodbye."

"Jas."

"What? Look, it's only twenty-four hours until Tom gets back and I—"

"OK, chocks away, Jas, I'm going in."

Two minutes later

Right, this is it. He has asked me out, so that must mean he wants me to go out with him. Unless the number he gave me was a safety-deposit-box number or his idea for a lottery number. Uh-oh, my brain has wandered off to Madland. Better get a grip.

Light, cheerful, with a hint of Eastern promise – that is what I must be.

Should I break the ice with a joke?

Yes, yes, that's a good idea. I'll just say, "*Ciao*, Masimo. It's me, Georgia. Hey, what is black and lies on top of the water shouting knickers? He will say in his lovely accent, "*Non capisco*, Georgia. What is black and lies on top of the *acqua* shouting knickers?" And I will say "crude oil". And he will laugh and I will laugh and it will be... er... a laughathon.

Good, good, excellent. And I will leave Sparta and Pope Joan out of it completely.

And pants.

Two minutes later

Phoned the number.

264

Oh noooooo, it was ringing. He might answer it. Ohhhhnoooo.

I slammed the phone down.

Calm calm calmy calm calm.

I was just about to try again, when the phone rang.

I picked it up and said, "Look, can you get off the phone? I am just about to make a very important phone call."

And Masimo said, "Georgia? Have you call me?"

Ohbloodyblimey.

I forgot about telling him the joke and made up some ludicrous story about me just having rung him when the doorbell rang and it was people collecting for Overseas Pants. I don't know why I said that, I just had pants on the brain from Dave the Laugh.

Anyway, I don't think he understood me because he still wants to go out with me.

It was gorgey and fabby to speak to him.

He has got a lovely voice on the phone.

He is going to meet me tomorrow at 7:30 at a little Italian restaurant that he knows.

Buennissimo!!!

Tuesday June 14th

The day dragged by. I started my make-up in double French. I could only risk nail varnish because if Madame Slack saw a hint of cover-up it would be off to the guillotine for me.

Ran home.

Operation Go on a Date with a Luuurve God and Not Make a Complete and Utter Prat of Myself

5:00 p.m.

My feet, thankfully, seem to be their normal selves again.

Dithering around in my room.

The phone has rung about forty million times from the Ace Gang asking me what I'm wearing. "Not much" is the answer, because I am too busy answering the phone.

6:30 p.m.

I can't dither around for much longer. For once my hair is quite nearly not useless, and I think my boots and skirt look good together. My feet fit into the boots as well, which is a plus.

I went downstairs as quietly as I could, but the Mad Committee were all there to see me off. All lined up by the door. Even Angus had come in from his canoodling with Naomi. He was in the kitchen coughing and choking and looking like he was being sick. Then I noticed that was because he had a frog in his mouth that he was trying to eat. How disgusting and mad is that? It was still alive as well. Mum got into her usual position on the table and screamed at Dad to chase him out. Gordy tried to snack on it and Angus just biffed him over the head. I took the opportunity to sneak out.

7:30 p.m.

I was sooooo nervy as I arrived at the restaurant. He was outside waiting for me. He is the best-looking person I have ever seen. Why would he like me? Maybe he feels sorry for me?

Maybe he's a Christian and he thinks I'm a bit mentally subnormal.

Yes, that might be it. He might be an Italian Lady Cliff Richard.

He smiled at me when he saw me and suddenly I felt like the most beautiful girl in the world. He said, "You came. I am so glad and happy."

He held the door open for me. It was very like what I imagine a grown-up feels like. The owner of the restaurant came over and said, "Good evening, Masimo, *come sta?*"

And they chatted in Italian. Then we went to our table. I sat down without smashing the chair to smithereens, which is a good start.

Ten minutes later

We have ordered our food and I think I very nearly haven't said anything too mad. Or maybe it's because Masimo doesn't speak English well enough to know that I am being a fule.

Twenty minutes later

Then I inadvertently started the pants scenario again. I am going to have to kill Dave the Laugh. The Pantsmeister. Stopit stopit.

Masimo said, "My home, my family, is Verona. So beautiful. I would like you to see it one day. It is where *Romeo and Juliet* was set."

I was chomping on pizza as he was talking. I was doing quite well, cutting it up very small so that I didn't have any bits falling out of my mouth, but then I momentarily broke my vow of sanity and quoted from *Romeo and Juliet*. I said, "Oh I love Rom and Jul, especially that bit when he compares her to the moon – you know, when he sees her and says, "But soft, what PANTS through yonder window breaks."

And then I started honking and snorting with laughter. Oh nooooooo.

Fortunately Masimo laughed as well. Not in a "quickly I'll get to the phone and someone keep her talking" sort of way. In a nice way. Like he really likes me.

An hour later

The meal was amazingly all right. I find him really easy to talk to. He is sort of in between Dave and the Guitar Plucker. I don't tell as many jokes and do stupidnosity with him as I do with Dave, but I don't get all tongue-tied and full of ludicrosity like I did with the Guitar Plucker.

I realised I was having a lovely time. I said a little inward thank-you prayer to Our Lord Sandra.

Then the snoggosity tension began to build. He touched my hand and looked into my eyes. His amber eyes have got

269

little flecky bits of deeper yellow in them. Oh blimey, we were doing sticky eyes. I could feel my brain trickling out of my head.

He said, "Your eyes, they are like a pussy cat that has drunk *vino rosso*."

So is that a good or bad thing?

I took it as good and tried to keep any image of cross-eyed Gordy out of my mind.

He paid for our pizzas and then he said, "Would you like to walk? It is a nice night. We could look at the stars together."

I resisted saying, "Twinkle twinkle little PANTS."

We walked along to the edge of town and on to the back fields. It was a lovely soft evening, and as we walked he said, "Are you *freddo*?"

Oh dear God! He wasn't going to talk about elves and hobbits, like boys did, was he?

But then he said, "I am sorry, I mean are you, er, in English... cold?"

I said, "Well, I..."

And he put his arm around me.

I was almost fainting with anticipation. My whole body

was on high snog alert. I wondered what he would do next.

He said, "Look, *cara*, a shooting star."

And we saw a shooting star. I wished very hard in my head for world peace, and to get to number six.

And it happened!!!

Not world peace, obviously, although you never know.

When I looked up at the shooting star he put his hand on my chin and gently turned my head towards his. Then he kissed me like he did the first time we saw each other. Just a little soft kiss. Like Jas's lezzie aunt's kiss.

I thought, *Oh no, here we go again on to the rack of love.* But then he kissed me again. A bit harder this time. It was soooo fab and groovy and gorge. I accidentally began singing that famous song from *The Sound of Music* in my brain. "The hills are alive with the sound of PANTS!" Shutup brain. And get out of my brain, Julie Andrews. You snog people in leather shorts if you like.

As my brain was burbling on to itself, Masimo changed his snogging technique. He began kissing my neck with little soft kisses. From the bit near my earlobes right down to near my collar bone and then back to my mouth. Wow and wowzee wowow! I turned into Melted-neck Girl.

I don't know how long we were out there in the field. And for one of the first times in my life my brain froze. I actually stopped thinking and just felt things. Oo-er. You see now I have started thinking again, but I didn't while he was kissing me.

He ran his hands through my hair. His lips were really soft and sort of firm at the same time. He was talking softly in Italian to me. And every now and again he would look me in the eyes. It was a bit like being hypnotised, but in a nice way.

We should put sticky eyes on the snogging scale I think because it's vair vair nice and groovy and full of the spirit of red-bottomosity.

I felt like all the blood had drained out of my body and I would have stayed there all night attached to his mouth. Then he nip libbled!! He could do nip libbling!!! Dave wasn't the only one who could do it. It was so nice and felt so good that I even had the courage to nip libble him, just a little mousey nibble but a nibble nonetheless. And he liked it. He did that moaney thing. Officially in my *How to Make Any Twit Fall in Love with You* it is the girl who is supposed to do the moaney stuff, but live and let snog I say.

We didn't bang teeth or anything. It was like a mouth dance. And I was Missvairgoodatmouthdancing!!!

And then it happened... number six!

He put just the tip of his tongue in my mouth. It was really sweet. I felt so full of luuurve for him that I put my tongue in his mouth a little bit. And our tongues touched!!! They were snogging as well!!! When you describe it it doesn't sound like it would be very nice, but it is. Perhaps that is why Angus and Gordy put the tips of their tongues out, because they know how sexy tongue touching can be.

No, on second thoughts, I know that they put their tongues out because they are idiot cats.

I was liking the kissing so much that I didn't even think about breathing. I had acquired David Blaineness – I could very possibly not breathe for weeks if the Luuurve God was kissing me.

But then he stopped. Boooooo, stop stopping!!! He said, "Come, Georgia, I must take you home. Your father will like it."

Bollocks to my vati. I wanted more snogging!!

I said, "What time is it? Er, I mean, *Che ora per favore?*"

Masimo gave me a big kiss on my cheek.

"*Mille grazie* for speaking my language. *Sono le dieci.*"

I said, "Ah. Good. Er, *buono*. Yes, marveloso all round."

He said, "You don't know what that is in time, do you?"

"No."

"It is ten o'clock."

Phwoar, we had been snogging for almost two hours. Yesss!!! I bet we had even out-snogged Rosie and Sven.

I said, "Vati said I didn't really have to be in especially at any time tonight. In fact, he said if I wanted to stay out all night that was fine by him."

Masimo put his arm round me. It felt fabby to be held by his lovely armio. "Georgia, I don't think that you are a fibber but maybe... just maybe you are insane."

Then he laughed. "Come on, bad girl. I take you home, your papa is pleased, he thinks I am the good guy, then we go out lots more, no?"

We walked home, stopping every few steps for more snogging. Unfortunately we didn't bump into anyone that I knew. Drat!!! Mind you, every girl that we passed gawped at Masimo. Shutup, gawpers, he is mine all mine mineio. I think.

I hadn't mentioned the Wet Lindsay scenario. In fact I

hadn't really asked him anything about girlfriends, even though I am dying to know.

He asked me about the Guitar Plucker though. He said, "And how do you feel about Robbie now? Do you still like him?"

Hmm. This called for diplomosity with just a hint of caringosity. Under no circumstances did I want him to think I was a minx who just picked up boys and tossed them aside... oo-er.

I said, "I like him as a friend now. He plays the guitar in streams."

Masimo looked at me and said, "I understand."

Which is a plus. And a surprise, actually, as I certainly don't make any sense to myself.

He kissed me at the gate, and he did that varying pressure thingy, and a quick kiss under my earlug... phwoar... and then he sort of shook his shoulders and sighed and said, "OK, *cara*, now we are sensible and good. Sad for me."

He took my hand and led me to my door and rang the bell. Vati came and answered the door. Oh blimey, he was Il Ministrone again. He NEVER smokes cigars, but he happens to be smoking one now. AGAIN. Also he has semi-proper trousers on, not his joggerbums, which make him look like Porkman.

He said, "Well, good, fine. Well, did you have a pleasant evening?"

I was about to say, "What in the name of arse has it got to do with you?"

But Masimo shook his hand!! And he said, "*Buona notte*, Mr Nicolson. Here is your lovely daughter home safe."

He turned to me and kissed my hand and said, "Thank you for a lovely evening. *Arrivederci* till the next time."

Vati went back indoors, shouting out, "*Arrivederci* then." He really does think we are in *The Sopranos*. He'll start having his mates "rubbed out" soon.

As I went through the door I looked after Mr Gorgeous. He turned round and winked at me and blew me a kiss. And he said, "*Subito*."

In bed, the bed of the Luuurve Goddess

He said "Subito" to me.

How fab is that?

Later

Actually, I don't know how fab it is, as I don't know what it means.

Ten minutes later

Something to do with submarines? I'll have to look it up in my *Idiots Guide to Italian*.

Fifteen minutes later

It means "soon".

That's a bit like "s'later", isn't it?

Oh dear God.

Wednesday June 15th

Walking along with Jas, trying to get a word in edgeways with Mrs Mad.

Tom is back on a flight at 6:15 p.m. That is 6:15 p.m. Do you get it? Not 6:00 p.m. but 6:15 p.m. And do you know how many minutes that is? I do. I have also become a Time Lord.

Jas was actually SKIPPING as we went along to Stalag 14. Dear *Gott in Himmel* I have got a lamb as a mate. She was saying, "OOOooooohhh, I am soooooo excited."

"Yes, I know you are. Look, can I just tell you about Masimo?"

"Do you think he will go home first and drop his bag off or come straight round to mine? I wonder what kind of pressies he has brought me from Kiwi-a-gogo land."

Hopeless trying to talk to her.

Break

Ace Gang meeting.

They all (apart from Jas who has gone off to the woods to "think"... I laughed at first when she said that, but then I realised she was serious)... anyway, what was I saying before... Oh yes, the whole Ace Gang wanted to know about my date.

Rosie said, "So dish the goss. What are our Pizza-a-gogo friends like in the snogging department?"

"Absobloodylutely fabby fab and marv."

Mabs said, "Really?"

"Yep, he did nip libbling, neck nuzzling, tongues, etc."

Ellen said, "Did he, you know, I mean did he..."

I said, "Yep."

Which seemed to satisfy her.

278

As the bell went Rosie said, "So when are you seeing him again? I mean is he the official boyfriend now?"

Hmmmmm. Good point, well made.

Last period

The Foxwood lads over again for *MacUseless*. Dave smiled at me when he ambled in. Ellen immediatedly dashed off to the loos to apply more lippy.

I wanted to tell him about Masimo, but before I could go and chat to him, Miss Wilson came in to give us her official loon on loon tablets address.

Ellen came in all tarted up and red and sat down near Dave.

Miss Wilson said, "Now then, let us get on with the production in the professional manner that I know you are all capable of."

3:30 p.m.

The witches were making so much racket doing their improvised dance round the fire bit that Hawkeye was attracted into rehearsals. She shouted at them from the door.

♥ 279

"Stop that idiotic prancing around immediately."

Rosie said, "It's our improvised witches' dance, Miss Heaton."

"I don't care what it is, I can hear it in the science lab."

I said to Miss Wilson after she had stormed off, "I don't think Miss Heaton quite appreciates the beauty of the Swan of Avon, Miss Wilson."

Rosie said, "You should tell her that you used to go out with him in the olden days."

Miss Wilson started getting all flustered. "Now, don't be silly, Rosie. Of course I did not go out with William Shakespeare..."

Dave joined in. "Why? Didn't he want to go out with you? Was he too busy or something? The Devil makes work for idle PANTS."

Then it was quite literally all pants from then on.

Miss Wilson finally called it a day when I said, "Macduff was from his mother's PANTS untimely ripped."

As we got our stuff from the cloakroom, Mabs said, "I saw Rachel in town and she is really really upset about her and Dave breaking up."

Ellen has been mooning around him in rehearsal. He's

been quite nice to her actually. I wonder if I would mind if he went out with her. I should, as a great mate, be really pleased if he did go out with her but... anyway.

Ellen and Dave were by the gates as we ambled out to go home. I am in such a good mood. Maybe Dave and she *should* go out again.

As I watched them Dave gave her a little kiss on her cheek and she went bright red. You could tell even from about two hundred yards away, and then Ellen tripped off home. Dave looked after her and then turned round and leaned on the gate. He was chatting to girls as they filed past him. He is a big flirt.

It was just Jas and me walking home because Rosie was off to see Sven for a quick four hour snog in the woods, and Mabs and Jools were going shopping.

Dave came with us as we walked along. I said to him, "Pantsmaster, can I tell you about Masimo?"

Dave looked at me. "Am I going to be able to stop you?"

As we were walking along Jas was saying, "Stop walking so slowly, you lot. Oh, I can't stand this." And she started running. She yelled at us, "I've only got two hours to do my make-up for Tom, coz he likes me just natural."

What was she talking about? As we watched her bottom disappear into the dusk, Dave said, "It's nice, really, isn't it, to be that simple?"

"What? You would like to be as stupid as Jas?"

"No, I mean Jas and Tom. They just like each other and that's it, no sign of the Cosmic Horn or red-bottomosity."

I could feel things getting a bit philosophical and I wanted to talk about snogging. "Dave, I was going to ask you about Mas—"

Dave said, "What if you were really meant to be with someone? But you kept messing about and having the Horn and so on and you lost them."

Oh, brilliant, Dave the Laugh was having one of his unlaugh moments.

Bugger, he had gone all girly. I was going to have to talk about his stuff before I was allowed to get on to the interesting stuff about me and the Italian Stallion.

I said really quickly, "Look, I'm sure that if you went back to Rachel she would forgive you, she is remarkably stup... er... stupendously nice."

Dave looked at me and said, "You just don't get it, do you?"

"Oh, you mean Ellen. She would have you back tomorrow; she has no pridenosity."

He said, "You great kittykat loonie. I am talking about you and me."

"Don't be daft."

Dave didn't say anything, and then he said, "The bigger the PANTS the harder they fall."

What?

The Big Furry Paw of Fate

In my room
5:30 p.m.
What was Dave the Laugh talking about? Besides the pants, I mean. Him and me? Losing the person meant for you. Has he snapped?

6:15 p.m.
Tom will just be landing now – Jas will have gone mad.

6:16 p.m.
Phone rang. It was Jas. I was right.

   "Gee, he's here – he is in the same land as me."

   Yeah, well, its debatable whether anyone normal is in the same land as Jas, but I let it go.

Amazingly she was prepared to talk about me.

She said, "I'm all ready so I'm going to talk to you and let you talk to me so that I don't go mad, because I reckon it will take about half an hour through customs, he may have brought back some interesting specimens of nature and that might hold him up, and then it will be another hour from the airport and then he might go to his house so that is about 8:30 p.m."

It is truly like talking to the speaking clock.

After we had been through the minutes business again Jas rather unexpectedly remembered that I was alive. "Georgia, you know Masimo?"

"Er... YES!"

"Well, I think you should be, you know, brave with him. I think you should just tell him how you feel and not do glaciosity or anything."

"Really?"

"Yes, I do, because then you would, you know, be like real and not a facsimile of a sham. I mean, even if you convinced him that you were normal, sooner or later you would forget and go back to being you."

"Er, Jas, this is not exactly—"

"It's like your nose, isn't it?"

"My nose?"

"Yes, I mean, say you wore like a nose disguiser."

A nose disguiser?

The strain has finally sent her over the edge.

I said, "You mean from the 'nose-disguiser' shop?"

"Whatever. Well, sooner or later he would discover that you had a big nose."

"It's a generous nose."

"You don't have to tell any of us that, Georgie. Anyway, what I'm saying is, I think you should be you because actually you are quite nice."

She put the phone down then because she decided to change her skirt and wear jeans because Tom might want to go on a ramble when he arrived home.

A ramble?

Be myself?

Not use glaciosity or visit the nose-disguiser shop?

I was feeling a bit unusual.

7:00 p.m.
I went downstairs and Mutti and Libbs were in the kitchen.

They both gave me big smiles when I came in. Mum said, "Hello, darling, you are getting so leggy and pretty and grown-up. Isn't your big sister gorgeous, Bibbity?"

Libbs was in the middle of putting Gordy's slippers on, but she looked up and said, "Hello my Gingey, I lobe you. Kiss Gordy."

I kissed a cat!

I really am losing my grip.

Mum said I was gorgey.

She looked at me as if she was going to cry.

8:30 p.m.

Blimey life is full of confusiosity. Suddenly everyone luuurves me. Dave the Laugh rambling on about what if we were meant to be together, the Guitar Plucker says he misses me... I've kissed Gordy. What next? Hawkeye apologising for confiscating my bison horns?

The phone rang.

Oh God!!! It can't be Hawkeye about the horns, surely!

I yelled downstairs, "Phone!!!"

Mum must be having the usual communal bath with Libby and Angus and Gordy because there was a massive amount of giggling and splashing and shrieking going on. Hang on a minute, there was a man's voice as well. Was Libby doing impressions?

Mum yelled, "Georgia, can you get that?"

I said, "I'm upstairs. Why can't Vati get it?"

Then Vati yelled up, "I'm all wet. You get it; it will be for you anyway."

Oh bloody hell.

As I went to get the phone I had to pass the bathroom and I saw something that may mean counselling for many many years. It was my father with no strides on!! I mean it! He was standing up in the bath, and Mum was in there and Libby, and they were all in the nuddy-pants!!! I almost choked.

I had seen my own father in the nuddy-pants.

With my mum in the nuddy-pants.

Together.

In the nudey-dudeys.

How horrific and unnatural was that?

Still in a state of shock, I answered the phone.

"Hello."

"*Ciao*, Georgia."

Masimo!!!

"I have been thinking about you. I will look forward to seeing you. Can you see me on Saturday?"

I said, "Well, yes that would be. I mean yes, erm..."

"If you can't wait to see me, you could, how you say... come tomorrow night. There is a gang of us going to Late and Live, you know, with Lindsay, like before. Can you come?"

I don't really remember what I said to him.

9:00 p.m.
Phoned Jas. Her mum said, "Hello, love, she's gone out with Tom for a bit of a ramble."

Good grief.

Phoned Rosie. "Rosie."

"Hubble bubble toil and pants."

"Rosie, this is serious. I just spoke to Masimo and you know you were asking me about the is-he-my-boyfriend scenario?"

"*Sí.*"

"Well he asked me out on Saturday, and then he said that if I wanted to see him before then he is going to Late and Live with the gang and Lindsay."

"Crikey."

9:30 p.m.
Phoned all of the gang and now I am really really teetering on the brink of bewildermentosity. I may be driven to talk to my mum again.

9:40 p.m.
I can't get the picture of her in the nuddy-pants out of my head.

I have managed to superimpose a pair of all-encompassing overalls on the mental image of my vati *vis à vis* the bathroom scenario. But I can't do it with Mum because bits of her basoomas keep re-emerging from anything I camouflage her with. Very like in real life.

10:30 p.m.
As it happened, she came up to my bedroom to say good night anyway.

As she was at the door I said, "Mum, if I tell you something, will you promise not to come over all mumish?"

She said, "I'll try. What's going on?"

I told her about the snogging – well, a bit, I skated over the details – well, in fact, I said, "it was a really nice night and he kissed me good night." I didn't go into the tongues and so on.

Then I told her about him phoning me and asking me out again and then the Lindsay bit.

She sat down on the bed. "Hmm. That is tricky, isn't it? I mean she could be just another mate. He doesn't know a lot of people yet, does he? Or maybe he doesn't want you to get the wrong idea about him being a serious boyfriend."

Oh buggery bum.

Then she thought a bit and said, "Do you know what I think? You have to decide what you want. Ask for it and either get it or, if he doesn't want the same thing as you, you have to accept it. Life is for the brave."

After she had gone I lay in the dark and thought about what she had said.

It was sort of what Jazzy Spazzy had said, even though she went on about the nose-disguiser shop. Even Dave the Laugh had said more or less the same thing.

Yes, well that was it. Ask for what I want and Devil take the hindmost. Good.

Midnight

Yes, but what do I want?

Thursday June 16th
Stalag 14
Love hell

Wet Lindsay seems to be everywhere I look today, adjusting her thong. I am sure she's looking at me as well. I wonder if she knows about me and Masimo? He must be in contact with her, otherwise how would he know that she's going to Late and Live? Also he gave her a lift home the other day. And how do I know how often he sees her anyway?

German

Even Herr Kamyer sitting on his glasses and then not being able to find them because they were stuck on his bottom couldn't cheer me up.

I have to make a decision. I can't go on like this.

Break

Jas is quite literally on Cloud Nine. On and on about Tom. I wanted to spoil it for her somehow. When she started skipping again (I am not joking, I wish I was) and going "Oh I am soooooo happy", I said, "So are you going to MARRY Hunky and never go out with anyone ever again? For the next fifty years?"

Jas said, "Well, if you found the right person what would be the point of going out with anyone else?"

I said, "Because he might not BE the right person; you might only THINK he was the right person."

"I do think Tom is the right person."

"Yeah, but he might not be."

"Yeah, but he is."

"Yes, but he might not be."

"But he is."

We could have done that for several hours.

7:30 p.m.
Anyway, I am not going to go to Late and Live tonight. The fact is that I am not really brave and sophisticated and a glacial minxy. If I saw Masimo getting off with Lindsay, or anyone else for that matter, I wouldn't like it A LOT. And that is a fact. I am a bit of a jelloid person and I want

someone to like me as much as I like them.

And I do like Masimo.

9:00 p.m.
Mooning around. They will be all at Late and Live now. Ooohhhh. I can't stand this.

9:30 p.m.
I can't even speak to Hornmeister Dave, because he said that odd thing the other day on the way home. Surely he isn't serious about me and him. I mean I really really like him. A LOT, and he does make me laugh but... ooohhhh God! It is all quite literally giving me the Cosmic droop.

9:40 p.m.
Went down into the front room. Angus and Gordy were grooming each other. They were both licking each other's heads with their tongues. Aaaah how vair sweet. They loved each other despite everything. Love conquers all. Look at Katheeeee and Heathcliff in *Wuthering Pants* and Jane Eyre and Rochester in *Jane's Pants* and so on.

Just then Gordy licked Angus's fur the wrong way and

Angus biffed him so hard he flew straight off the sofa and into the wastepaper basket.

Vati is out with his lads' army. They have taken up roller skating now and go to this roller dome place where other complete prats career around injuring themselves.

I said to Mum, "I am convinced there is a book called *How to be the Most Embarrassing Dad in History* and it has hints like "Grow an amusing novelty moustache", "Wear leather trousers", "Talk bollocks in front of your teenage daughter's friends", "Pretend to be Il Ministrone", "Adopt a hobby – roller skating or clown-car racing are particularly good".

Anyway, I slumped down on the sofa and Angus got on my knee and started doing that kneading thing they do to make you all comfy. For them. I am like a human bean bag to him. Mum came and sat next to me. She even touched my arm. I let her though because I am too tired to do anything about it.

She said, "You know what you were asking me last night? Well, this is what I think... I think you are not a two-timey sort of person really, it makes you anxious and upset and hell to be with, frankly. Soooo... even though you might be

♥ 295

with a person only for a bit, I think you should take that bit seriously so that you act nicely and get the best out of it. And if you have to say goodbye or they have to say goodbye some time, well that is life, and good training for you both for when the right person comes along."

Blimey.

That was almost full of wisdomosity. If I could figure out what in the name of arse she was on about.

I said, "Let me get this, you think I should tell Masimo that I want to be like a girlfriend and boyfriend, and if he doesn't want to then I should probably not see him?"

She nodded.

Crikey, this was all a bit radical.

I liked it when I was led around by the Horn.

When did this acting with maturiosity happen?

Friday June 17th
School

Wet Lindsay was unbearable today. I am sure she is stalking me. Everywhere I went, there she was. I went into the canteen and was sitting there minding my own business, looking through my *MacUseless* script, when she came in with ADM and another complete loser called Rowena. There were loads of spare chairs to sit on but, oh no, they had to come and sit on the table next to me. Lindsay looked at me like I was a snot creature having my snot lunch. Then they started talking.

Lindsay said, "It was groovy last night, wasn't it? I think it is such a cool venue, and there is an older crowd so you don't get all the crap dancing and useless behaviour. I'm tired again though, it's such a late night midweek and Mas is, you know, well, you know what he is like. Italians, eh?"

And she laughed sort of knowingly and they all joined in.

I couldn't stand this. I got up and walked off.

I wonder if I could just kill her accidentally.

4:10 p.m.

I was waiting at the gate for Jas. she was still dithering around in the loos doing her lippy.

Tom came to meet Jas after school and it was really really nice to see him. He does look a lot like his brother.

He hugged me.

"Georgie how are you? Beyond groovy to see you."

He snogged Jas when she came puffing up. She must have

spent the last class doing her fringe because it looked very nearly normal.

We walked along together. Jas was all over him like a rash. It was vair nice to have him back. He told us all about Kiwi-a-gogo land.

"When you leave they don't say 'goodbye', they say 'hurrah'."

I said, "That seems a bit rude."

Tom said, "I rest my case. I did have a great time though. We did loads of water sports. Surfing and white-water rafting. There is an amazing range of flora and fauna there."

I looked at him. He laughed. "No, perhaps I won't tell you about the wombats. Robbie sends you his love. He said he hadn't heard from you. And he would really like it if you would write back."

Jas looked at me in a "I told you so" way. I hope she is not going to be even more of a Wise Woman of the Forest now that Hunky is back; it is the last thing I need.

There was a bit of an awkward pause. Then Tom said, "Look, Georgia, Robbie is my brother and I love him."

(Hang on, what is going on with blokes? Mincing on about their feelings. There is none of this stuff in *Men are from Knob land Women are from Pink Frilly land* book.)

Tom saw my face and said, "No, Georgia, I am not on the turn. What I mean is, he left you and you can do anything you like. All I am doing is passing on a message. Anyway, I hear there have been developments on the Italian Stallion front."

Radio Jas pretended to be checking her bag.

5:00 p.m.
Jas and Tom left me at Jas's gate and walked up her path with their arms around each other. I felt a bit lonely for my pal. Now that Tom was back I wouldn't have her to myself any more, and I thought about the times in Hamburger-a-gogo land and the nuddy-pants scenario.

Rosie had Sven. Mabs seems to be keen on Tosser's mate, Jools sort of has Rollo, and even Ellen is keen on one of the backstage *MacUseless* people. I was beginning to be a spinster of the parish.

5:10 p.m.
I wandered off lonely as a clud once more and as I walked along I got my mirror out of my rucky and looked in it. OK,

I wasn't the most beautiful girl in the world but I had a nice face (ish) and Masimo had said he liked my eyes. Mind you, who knows what he had said to Lindsay. Surely not "Oh, *cara*, you have the *buenissimo* tiny forehead."

I put on a bit of lippy and mascara and eyeliner. I would do a bit of hip waggling and flicky hair to cheer myself up. Amazingly, almost immediately a boy leaned out of a car window and went, "Niiiiiice."

Crikey, a bit of lippy and hip waggling and you could rule boyworld. How vair vair superficial they were. On the other hand I liked a good-looking boy myself, and I liked nice hair and I liked Masimo's clothes and scooter. I wouldn't like him just for that though.

Everything is vair vair confusing.

5:20 p.m.

I was crossing the road for home when Masimo sped round the corner on his scooter and came to a halt next to me. He got off and took his helmet off quickly. He didn't say anything, he just came over to me and snogged me. A proper number five. There in the middle of the street.

Oscar and his mates were slouching along trailing their

ruckies on the ground, walking backwards and shouting, the usual boy stuff. When they saw Masimo snog me they all went, "Come on, my son, get in there!!"

And so on. Sensationally mad.

Masimo didn't even notice them. He stopped kissing me and held me at arms' length. "You didn't come last night. I missed you."

I felt all flustered and red and before I could think I blurted out, "Did you? Why? Wasn't Lindsay enough for you?"

Masimo sat down on his scooter seat.

"Georgia, tell me what is all this?"

So I blabbed everything out. Things I didn't even know I was going to say. In other words rubbish probably. Anyway, I told him that I wasn't cut out for callous sophisticosity.

"I know that Dave the Laugh says that we are young and we hear the call of the Horn, and it is true, but I would give up the Horn to see how I felt properly."

Masimo looked a bit puzzled. "The Horn?"

"You know, like red-bottomsity."

"Red-bottomosity."

"You know, when you said you had been burned in the

oven of life and you just wanted to live in Fun City. But I don't want to live in Fun City. Well I do. But not with anyone, just with... anyway. That's what I mean."

Masimo laughed. Crikey, he had a nice laugh.

"Oh, now I see, Signorina Georgia. You are saying you would like me to be your boyfriend."

Blimey.

Now he had said it.

I went all red and stupid.

"Well. I suppose, yes I am. I'm sorry."

He was just looking down at the ground.

Oh God, what had I done?

I tell you what I had done, I had listened to my stupid mother, who hadn't spoken a word of sense since Henry VII was alive. I had listened to someone who couldn't control her breasts. Ohgodohgodohgoddygod. I was a fool.

I had to say something because Masimo was so quiet. I said, "Look, look forget it. I am sorry, *mi dispiace*. I well... it's just me, and you were not even thinking about... oh look, please forget what I said. I just can't do casualosity. It must be something in my genes."

Masimo did look up then.

"You have something in your jeans?"

"No. Look, oh, blimey I had better go. I have a bath to fill and a bottle of gin to buy."

I was about to start crying, I knew it, so I started to cross the road. And Masimo was just sitting there not saying anything.

I got into my house and just leaned against the door shaking. What had I done?

Angus and Gordy were sitting on the top of the bedroom stairs looking at me. Angus was biffing something around with his paw. Some poor little woodland creature, or a spider or something. I knew what it felt like to be biffed around by the big furry paw of fate.

In my room

Oh Goddy God's panties.

The letter from SG was still on my dressing table where I had left it. Another reminder of someone else I had lost. Why did he have to write to me now? I looked at his picture. Did he have to be so gorgey, even when I was eschewing him with a firm hand and had put him in the basket of yesterday? Why was I even bothered? I suppose it was

♥ 303

because he was my first true love.

Ohhh booo.

I will NOT cry.

Why did all this happen to me? Had I really been a wasp in a former life, like Jas said?

Five minutes later

They say you always remember your first snog. And that is what he was. I was a snogging virgin until he came along with his guitar plucking.

Two minutes later

Well, he was my first PROPER snog. No one could be expected to count Whelk Boy, unless you were some kind of pervert who liked molluscs.

One minute later

I wonder where the SG's tape is that he made for me when I came back from Froggy land.

I think I put it at the back of my top drawer out of Libby's reach, with my boy entrancers and special-occasion knickers.

Two minutes later

I've found the tape, but where are my boy entrancers and special-occasion knickers? Dad's probably borrowed them.

One minute later

Put Robbie's tape on. I am full of nervosity because I do not want to be on the rack of love for him again. I am already on one rack.

Three minutes later

"Oh no, it's me again" about Vincent Van Gogh remains the most depressing song ever written. SG was not tip-top on the hilariosity front.

Gorgey though.

How full of confusiosity life is.

Two minutes later

Looking out of my window at the empty streets of life. Why does nothing ever go right for me? I could see Mr Next Door gardening in his enormous shorts. He could have a small African nation in them and you would never know. But he has Mrs Next Door to love him, shorts and all. And does he ever go looking for another Mrs Next Door? No he does not. He has big enough shorts to accomodate big red-bottomosity, but he does not use them.

Then I saw Mark Big Gob coming up the street with his lardy mates and with his arm around yet another tiny girl. Why does he like tee tiny girls? More to the point, why do they like him? How could anyone in their right mind snog him?

one minute later

Hang on a minute! Erlack, I'd managed to forget about him resting his hand on my basooma. Get out of my brain!!!

Four minutes later

Oh, Masimo, what have I done? Why did I listen to my stupid mother? I never normally do. She may have ruined my future happiness with her "just be yourself" bollocks. Dave the Laugh warned me, he said that you had just come out of a serious relationship and only wanted to have fun. Why can't I just live in Fun City and not be bothered about Being Really Me City?

What does Dave the sodding Laugh know about it

anyway? He has just finished with Rachel and before that he dumped Ellen. He is a serial heartbreaker.

Although he hasn't broken my heart yet.

In fact he has only ever been a bit mean to me when I used him as my red herring to attract the Sex God.

How many times have I accidentally snogged him? He is a good snogger, it has to be said.

Three minutes later
What did he mean about me and him? He's just my mate. And occasional snog buddy.

Ohhhh. I will never be happy again.

Or eat again.

One minute later
Not that there is ever anything to eat in this place anyway.

In the kitchen
Oh joy unbounded, there is a bit of leftover cold sausage.

What did Dave the Laugh say that really made me laugh when we were doing the battle scene in *MacUseless*? Oh, i know. He was waving a sword around (very nearly cutting off Melanie Griffiths' nungas) and shouting "Pants, pants! My kingdom for some pants!!!"

He is a vair funny person.

In my room

Well, why couldn't I just like Dave?

But then I thought of my night with Masimo when we had looked at the stars together, and I felt like crying.

If only I had had a chance to get to know him, I could have found out all about a different culture. I could have found out about neck snogging and everything. But I had well and truly blown it now. Wet Lindsay will be dancing about on her stick-insect legs when she finds out. Which she is bound to because of Radio Jas.

I wonder if I should phone Jas up and see what she thinks?

Am I mad? I might just as well phone Mrs Mad in Maddingtonshire.

Then I heard the familiar roar of a scooter engine below my window.

The doorbell rang.

I knew I should go and answer the door, but I couldn't

move my legs. Oh, marvellous, I was paralysed! Come on, come on legs, be brave, don't let me down now.

Hahahahahha, I was telling myself really crap inward jokes. Hurrah!

I eventually managed to stagger downstairs.

Oh, *mon Dieu*, I hope I don't inadvertantly go to the poo parlour division.

For confidence I picked up cross-eyed Gordy. He was busily chewing something so he didn't attack me.

I opened the door.

Masimo was there.

Oh God.

He looked at me and his eyes looked so soft and sad.

"Georgia. This is a big thing. Give me a little time. I will see you in a week and I will say yes or no. I will not, how you say. I will not mess about with you. I will say yes or no. *Ciao, cara.*"

And he blew me a kiss and got on his scooter and accelerated off.

I shut the door and stood there holding on to Gordy.

What had I done?

Gordy looked up at me, eye to eyes, and I looked down at

him. He looked at me as if he could see deep into my soul and understood. He even stopped chewing the spider thing he had in his mouth.

And suddenly I understood as well.

It wasn't a spider he was eating...

...And then he ate my boy entrancers.

Georgia's Glossary

boy entrancers · Ah yes. The re-emergence of the boy entrancers. Hmmm... well... boy entrancers are false eyelashes. They are known as boy entrancers because they entrance boys. Normally. However, I have had some non-entrancing moments with them. For instance, the time I used too much glue to stick them on with. It was when I was at a Stiff Dylans gig trying to entrance Masimo. I was intending to do that looking up at him and then looking down and then looking up again, and possibly a bit of flicky hair (as suggested in *How to Make Any Twit Fall in Love with You*). I did the looking-at-him-and-looking-down thing, but when I tried to look up again I couldn't, because my boy entrancers had stuck to my bottom lashes. So my eyes stayed shut. I tried raising my eyebrows (that must have looked good) and humming, but in the end, out of sheer desperadoes, I said, "Oooh, I love this one..." and went off doing blind disco-dancing to Rolf Harris's "Two Little Boys". So, in conclusion, boy entrancers are good, but be alert for glue extravaganzas.

chokey · A prison cell. Also known as pokey. Maybe because they are quite small cells.

chuddie · Chewing gum. This is another "i" word. We have a lot of them in English due to our very busy lives, explaining stuff to other people not so fortunate as ourselves.

David Blaine · For Heaven's sake, don't you know who he is? He's from New York, New York. He stands in blocks of ice for a year without food, and steals peoples watches. He came to England and hung around in a glass cage over Tower Bridge for a month. No one knows why.

fule · Fool. This is a more pleasant way of saying it (ish). It sounds more Christmassy, somehow... "Let's all go sing, a hey nonny no, and bring in the Christmastide fule for the fire", and so on.

hangi · in Kiwi-a-gogo land when Maoris have a picnic, they don't bother lugging sandwiches, flasks and so on; they get some beer and drink it, then they dig a big hole and put hot coals in it, then they chuck in six hundred pounds of sausages, eight sheep, hu hu bugs, etc. Then they fill in the hole with earth and leave it to cook all afternoon. The Maoris chat and play poi poi, then they dig up the food and tuck in. Yum yum. (Unless you get a hu hu bug, in which case erlack a pongo.)

Immac · A cream you use to remove evidence of the orang-utan gene. Hair remover.

Land of the Big White Clots · Now I am glad you asked me this, because it is a hilarious play on words. (It is, believe me.) Anyway, this is it. Kiwi-a-gogo land is called something in Maori that translates as "Land of the

Big White Clouds". But I have changed "clouds" to "clots" to hilarious effect, because it implies that Kiwi-a-gogo land is full of clots. Hahahahahahahhaha!

Oh dear God, you don't know what clots are, do you? I can feel my life ebbing away. But as it's you and I love you so much, I'll go on. Clots is an olde Englishe worde for "fool" i.e., a person who is in between a twit and a tosser.

laters · plural of s'later. Really, if I was being a nit-picking swotty-knickers (i.e., Jas) I would always say "laters" when I said s'later to the Ace Gang because they are plural. However, I am not Jas (hurrah!), so I say what I like.

O.A.P. card - stands for Old Age Pensioner card. This is a card to identify the elderly mad in our midst. It's supposed to mean that they show their card and get on buses for free and get cheap tickets at the cinema and so on, but really it's to alert people to their presence so that they can be ejected when they start causing trouble. You know the sort of thing – rattling their sticks and clacking their boiled sweets against their false teeth in the quiet bits of the film.

oeuvre · Now this means... er... hang on a minute, maybe it IS the french plural for eggs? Now you've got me all confused. *Un oeuf*, two *oeufs*... it's not two *oeuvre*, is it? Any fool would know that. Yes, I am pretty sure that it means "work", as in work of art. And not egg. Look, just leave it.

phased · A bit put out by something. Full of confusiosity and redness, and inward mayhem.

Pizza-a-gogo land · Masimoland. Land of wine, sun, olives and vair vair groovy Luuurve Gods. Italy. The only bad point about Pizza-a-gogo land is their football players, who are so vain that if it rains they all run off the pitch so that their hair doesn't get ruined.

quiff · You put some gel on your hair and make the front bit stick up in a wave. Elvis had one.

red-bottomosity · Having the big red bottom. This is vair vair interesting *vis à vis* nature. When a lady baboon is "in the mood" for luuurve, she displays her big red bottom to the male baboon. (Apparently he wouldn't have a clue otherwise, but that is boys for you!) Anyway, if you hear the call of the Horn, you are said to be displaying red-bottomosity.

score · Twenty pounds. (You are obsessed with money.) Score is a numbering system from Henry VIII's times. "Three score year and ten" meaning 70 years. The Hamburger-a-gogo types have no idea of the amount of words we have to remember in our land. They are very lucky that they made up their own language and can miss letters out – like aluminum and 'erbs instead of aluminium and herbs and so on.

sidies · Bits of face hair that men grow down the sides of their ears to their chins. If you are asking me why, try asking the Hamburger-a-gogo people, as I believe you will find George Washington started it.

slag · Slag is a lovely, complimentary word for girls, meaning madam. No it's not, it's a word that means "you are a rough, common, tarty girl with very low moral standards".

spangelfurkel · A kind of German sausage. I know. You couldn't make it up, could you? The German language is full of this kind of thing, like *lederhosen* and so on. And *Goosegot*. Vair vair good value.

squid · In English currency a pound is called a quid. (I don't know why, to be frank with you, but what I do know is that it is nothing to do with Harry Potter and quidditch, so don't even go there.) Squid is the plural of quid, and i do know why that is. A bloke owed another bloke six pounds or six quid and he goes up to him with an octopus with one of its tentacles bandaged up, and he says, "Hello, mate, here's the sick squid I owe you." Do you see? Do you see?? Sick squid – six quid??? The marvellous juxtaposition of... Look, we just call pounds squids. Leave it at that. Try and get on with people.

strop · A strop is number three on the famous "losing it" scale. This is as follows:

1. minor tizz

2. complete tizz and to do

3. strop

4. a visit to Strop Central

5. FT (funny turn)

6. spazattack

7. complete ditherspaz

8. nervy b (nervous breakdown)

9. complete nervy b

10. ballisiticisimus

truncheon · A fat piece of wood for policemen to bop criminals on the head with, or twirl about for a laugh. I have been told (by Jas so I am not relying on it), that the Hamburgese say "baton". But why their policemen have the time to conduct orchestras at work, I do not know.

updated snogging scale · Jas had a nervy b when I suggested adding "sticky eyes" as number one on the snogging scale. She said that would mean that everything else had the wrong number and that we would not know whether we had done number six or not, and so on. I said, "You speak for yourself, Jas. If someone sticks their tongue in my mouth, I will be the first to know." But, anyway, as she went sensationally red I came up with my expected stroke of geniosity. "Sticky eyes" is number a half on the snogging scale and "neck nuzzling" (mmmmm – dreamy) slips in (oo-er) at six and three quarters.

Turn the page for a sneaky peek
at my next book...

'...startled
by
his
furry
shorts!'
Fab New Confessions of
Georgia Nicolson
Louise Rennison

www.georgianicolson.com

Friday June 17th
on the rack of romance

And also in the oven of luuurve.

And possibly on my way to the bakery of pain.

And maybe even going to stop along the way to get a little cake at the cakeshop of agony.

Shutup brain shutup.

9:01 p.m.

In my bedroom looking out of my window at the stars.

It says in my *Meditation for Fools* book that it is very soothing looking at the universe and stars and everything.

Ommmm.

9:03 p.m.

God stars are annoying. Winking and blinking like twinkly idiots. No wonder they are so cheerful: they know nothing of the call of the Horn and snogging. They don't know what it is like to be me. Does anyone tell them to get into their PE knickers and rush about getting red? No. Do Luuurve Gods say, "I will let you know in a week's time if I want to go out with you or not."? No.

9:03 and a half p.m.
Anyway what are they actually for? You can't even read by them. They just hang about. Like dim torches.

9:07 p.m.
Oh brilliant! Every grey cloud has an even greyer lining; I can hear the powerful sound of a battery-driven Loonmobile. Hurrah the Swiss Family Mad are back! Still, my door is shut and it is quite obvious that I want a bit of privacy. That is what a closed door implies.

9:08 p.m.
That and the notice on it that reads KEEP OUT EVERYONE AND THAT MEANS YOU VATI.

9:10 p.m.

Oh good. My darling little sister has kicked open my door and flung Angus at me.

"HEGGOOOO Gingey!!! We is back. Heggo!! Watch my panties dance. Sex bum, sex bum, am a sex bum!!!"

Oh dear *Gott* in *Himmel*. Angus was livid at being thrown and once he'd stopped doing that cat sneezing and shaking thing he dug his claws into my ankle. Owwwwwww. Now I'm on the way to the cakeshop of aggers with a gammy leg. Hurray!!!

Libby put her frock over her head and waggled her botty around like a pole dancer. Where does she see people doing these things?

Then Mum came mumming in and scooped up Bibbs.

"Time for Boboland young lady."

Libby carried on singing and wiggling around in Mum's arms, and then Mum noticed me. Being in my bedroom.

"What are you up to, Georgia? Why are you in here?"

I said, "Not that anyone notices but this is actually my room. You know, for ME being in. I was in bed as it happens."

Mum said as she went out, "Oh you must be sooo tired,

all that lip gloss and mascara to carry round all day."

Vair vair amusing. Not.

9:25 p.m.
I've been in my bedroom for two hours since Masimo left me at my door saying he would let me know if I was his girlfriend or not. Why did I admit I wanted him to be like my proper boyfriend? Why why?

9:26 p.m.
And also thrice why? Whywhywhy? Why couldn't I have just been a callous sophisticate? Why? I could for once have just shut up and been all full of casualosity and *savoir* whatsit.

9:30 p.m.
If I'd played my cards right I could have had loads of boyfriends. All at the same time. Masimo the Italian Stallion for a weekendy boyfriend, with a touch of Dave the Laugh for a rainy weekday. And also maybe even have the former Sex God (whose name I wasn't going to mention even beyond the grave) as a sort of Kiwi-a-gogo airmail

boyfriend. But oh no I had to moan on about wanting to be Masimo's one and only.

9:40 p.m.

I was so happy snogging Masimo under the stars on our date. Stars didn't get on my nerves then. Nothing did.

Saturday June 18th

11:40 p.m.

I'm going mad. In fact things are so sheer desperadoes that I am going to have to phone the Big Knickered One and hope she doesn't ramble on about bat droppings.

Phoned Jas.

"Jas?"

"Sorry I'm out at the moment."

"Jas, please don't try and be amusing. Just be yourself. I have something *sehr schiessenhausen* to tell you."

"What have you done now? Stuck your toe up the bath tap?"

"Jas, I—"

"Thought it would be funny to paint a false moustache on your face but did it with indelible ink?"

"Jas I—"

"Shaved one side of your hair off?"

"Jas, shut up!!! Have you finally and completely snapped? Why would anyone paint a false moustache on their face with indelible ink?"

"I don't know. Why would anyone shave off their eyebrows?"

"Well, that was different, as you know I was using Vati's razor and—"

"Why would anyone go to a party dressed as a stuffed olive and paint their head and neck red as the stuffed pimento bit?"

"Actually, Jas, that was your idea – the stuffed bit. I was only thinking of being an olive, it was you that—"

"Why would anyone stick their false eyelashes together so that they couldn't open their eyes and then go dancing off to Rolf Harris's 'Two Little Boys'?"

"Jas, I really hate you when Tom gets back, you are so full of yourself."

I was absolutely full of lividosity, but she was so much in Jas 'n' Tom land that she didn't even notice I was going to kill her when I saw her. She just went on rambling for Europe.

"Oooh it's so groovy that he's back! I only saw him briefly yesterday. Only eight short hours but he is going to bring around his flora collection from Kiwi-a-gogo land in a bit and that will be sooo... oh..."

"Indescribably dull?" I said.

She said, "I have to go now."

"Jassy Wassy, can I come and see you? I need your help."

"No."

Jas's bedroom
3:00 p.m.

I am lying amongst Jas's sad collection of stuffed toys, mostly owls, while she ponces around in front of a mirror. What is she doing?

I said, "Jas it's very distracting trying to tell you stuff, important stuff full of tragicosity about me, your very bestest pally, when you keep pouting like a goldfish. What are you doing?"

"I'm practising puckering."

"What?"

"Puckering. I had, well, a bit of a problem *vis à vis* snogging with Tom last night."

Despite my world coming apart at the seams I am always interested in snogging tales.

"Tell me."

"Well, I was quite nervy at first when I was waiting for him."

"Were you doing your annoying flicky fringe thing?"

"I don't know... anyway, when he came in I was sort of jelloid. But then it was all right because he got his whatsits out."

"Pardon?"

"His, you know, snapshots from Kiwi-a-gogo land. As we were looking at them Tom got closer to me and put his arm around me. Then we... well... we, you know, started snogging and so on."

"And so on? What number did you get to?"

"Er... five and a bit of six. It was really groovy, I felt like I was all melting in to him and then... well... then I had sort of a lip spasm."

"A LIP SPASM???"

"Well I got cramp in my lips and they sort of seized up?"

"What does that look like?"

And she showed me. Blimey. You know when you put food in a baby's mouth and they don't like it and their eyes go all goggly and then their whole face goes into a spasm and the food comes shooting out of their mouth? Well even if you don't know, believe me I do. Libby could make rice pudding reach the other side of the room.

While Jas was showing me her spazzy face I said, "If you don't mind me saying, Jas, that is not very attractive."

She said, "I expect it was snogging withdrawal. I hadn't puckered up for ages so, you know, I was out of practice. But it won't happen again."

"Good."

"Because I have an exercise regime now. Shall I show you?"

"No."

"OK. It goes pucker, relax, pucker, relax, pucker, relax. Do you see?"

I didn't say anything, I just lay there staring at her with big starey eyes like the rest of the owls as she pouted her lips and then relaxed them. She looked like a mixture of Mick Jagger and an idiot. Not necessarily in that order.

She was in full ramble mode now.

"And then for the pièce de résistance it's darty tongue, darty tongue."

God it was horrible sitting there while her little tongue went in and out like a mad vole. Fortunately I was able to shove a Midget Gem in her gob so that I could continue with the sad tale of my Italian Stallion.

10 minutes later

She said (chewy chew), "So you said that he had to be your one and only boyfriend scenario or else that was it? *Arrivederci* Masimo?"

I said, "Yes, but—"

"Well, what in the name of Slim's outsize pyjamas were you thinking of? Are you mad?"

"No I'm not mad, Jas, I just happen to have a friend who looks a lot like you who said, 'Just be yourself.'"

"What?"

"You said being yourself and genuine was like having a generous nose. Like I have got. The exact words used were, 'Just because you have a generous nose, don't go to the nose-disguiser shop, let your own nose run free and wild.'"

"What complete fool said that?"

"YOU did, Jas."

"Did I? Well yeah, but I didn't mean it, did I? Clearly.

That was in the sanctity of our own brains, wasn't it? I mean we were going to the PRETEND nose-disguiser shop. I didn't actually mean you should BE yourself. That is just stupid."

I really really could kill her. In fact if I just attacked her stupid fringe suddenly she might choke on her stupid Midget Gem and that would be good.

Sadly Jas had got interested now. She said, "So let me get this right – he's choosing between you and Wet Lindsay? Blimey, does she know that? Because if she does you are dead as a doughnut. Deader."

Cheers.

Back in my bedroom of pain
9:30 p.m.

I had better plan what I am going to wear the day he comes round to see me. It may be the deciding factor between happiness and sadnosity.

I must make sure he doesn't see me in my school uniform: it will only remind him that I go to school.

9:40 p.m.

Oh what larks, I think I may be developing a lurker on my chin. Perfect, it should just be nicely ripening into a massive red puss-filled second chin by this time next week. I must take evasive action.

Five minutes later

I think you are supposed to draw lurkers out with ye olde poulticey thingy so that they come to a head quickly. What can I use as a poulticey type thingy?

In the bathroom

I have just looked in the "medical chest" and it has got some mouldy old oranges, a leg from Libby's Pantalitzer doll and some dried cat poo in it. How disgusting.

Mutti and Vati's bedroom

I've found some corn plasters in a drawer. Maybe they would do. I'll stick one over the top of the lurker.

Before I do I'll just squeeze it a bit to see if I can get anything out.

Five minutes later

Bloody hell now it really does hurt. And it's redder than Jas's head when she gets her enormous knickers in a twist. And that is very very red believe me. What can I do to calm it down. Maybe it needs something to dry it up – something with alcohol in it...

Sherry. Would that be good?

Two minutes later

Oh that is disgusting and sticky.

One minute later

Vati's aftershave has got alcohol in it. I'll try a dab.

Owwwwww buggering hells biscuits!!! Ow and owwy ow ow!

Ow.

Two minutes later

I'll put the corn plaster on now.

Well that is attractive. Not.

But who said that love was painless?

11:00 p.m.

God the lurker is throbbing. I hope the corn plaster isn't drawing anything else out. I don't want to wake up with no chin.

One minute later

Loony alert.

Bang bang crash. Why can no one in my family open a door normally. Crashing around when starving people with two chins are trying to sleep!

I heard Dad say, "Good grief! What is that smell?"

Mum said, "It's coming from Georgia's room."

Oh please leave me alone.

Dad yelled up the stairs, "I know that smell, it's my expensive aftershave. GEORGIA, WHAT THE HELL HAVE YOU BEEN UP TO NOW?"

Oh dear Lord. Rave on…